IN THE SHADOW OF THE LARK

In the Shadow of the Lark

LIVVY HOLLIS

IngramSpark

IngramSpark

In the Shadow of the Lark by Livvy Hollis
Published by IngramSpark

Cover design by Nissa Sykes
ISBN: 978-0-578-84169-4

First Printing, 2021

For my husband, Nathaniel; thank you for always listening to me ramble on about my story (like you had a choice).

For my grandmother, Brigitte, for bringing Faerie tales to life for me as a child.

and for my son, Henry James, who opened my heart to a completely different kind of magic.

September 1996

The piercing cries of newborn babies were carried through the castle halls on the warm breeze of a late Summer night. Charlotte smiled, her heart full with joy. A daughter had not been born to the royal family of Lark's Valley in decades and tonight they had been blessed with two!

Charlotte's happiness soon melted into worry. She sighed as she watched the Faerie Queen's carriage make its way across the stone bridge leading to their castle. There would be no time to celebrate as Grandma Charlotte. Right now she could only be Charlotte: Queen of Lark's Valley. She knew a visit from her neighbor, the Fae Queen, was never lighthearted.

"Does she not know we are not accepting visitors at the moment?" Her husband, King Phillip, grumbled.

"Perhaps she has come to offer her congratulations." Charlotte knew this wasn't true before she had even begun to utter the words.

Phillip knew it too. He scoffed, throwing his hands in the air and turning for the door, "well let's get this over with. We will see what she wants and send her on her way."

Queen Charlotte and King Phillip, who wanted nothing more than to spend time with their son, his wife, and their new granddaughters, reluctantly granted the trusted Fae prophetess and the Queen an audience in the throne room.

The uneasy feeling in Charlotte's stomach intensified, her mouth running dry, when she saw the grave expressions on the Faerie's faces as they sauntered across the marble floors. Charlotte was now certain that not only was this going to be unpleasant, but also much worse than they had first anticipated. One glance at her husband and it was clear that their thoughts were in the same place.

Her gut feeling was proved right. The prophetess was at least polite enough to quickly curtsy before telling of her vision.

"If allowed to remain together," her high voice shook, "one day the new twin girls will bring on the end of the world."

With every word, the joy in Charlotte's heart fluttered away. Everyone knew there was no doubting the prophetess; she had never been wrong before. Charlotte stole a glance at Phillip, whose face was growing redder with anger every second.

The Fae Queen calmly stepped forward; it was clear she was eager to address the King with a demand.

"I can promise you," her low voice slow and thick with disdain, "I will immediately rescind the peace treaty I formed with your ancestors if you do not do something to take control of this situation. The years of amity and harmony we have had will be but a faint memory. I will do whatever is necessary to save our world, if you will not."

"What would you have me do?" the King asked angrily, "they are infants; only hours old! How much harm could they be?"

"One must die." The Fae Queen stated boldly. "For the sake of our world."

Charlotte jumped in shock as Phillip launched himself from his throne, "absolutely not! How dare you suggest such a thing?"

She reached up to hold her husbands arm. "Now, now," Charlotte spoke much more calmly than she truly felt as she slowly rose from her seat.

Keeping her hand firmly on the King's forearm—could he feel her trembling?—she met the Fae Queen's gaze.

"Surely we will be able to discuss this peacefully and come up with a solution that appeases everyone involved. Let us meet again tomorrow after having some time to think on this news you've delivered us."

Charlotte let out a small sigh of relief as the Fae Queen silently agreed with a nod of her head before taking her leave.

* * *

The next morning as Charlotte and Phillip spent hours with their closest advisers discussing the difficult topic, Prince Charles paced in his wife's bedroom. Her chestnut hair was unkempt, but beautiful as always, while she nursed their daughters with a worried look in her cerulean eyes.

"Surely your mother and father won't allow harm to come to our daughters?" She asked.

"Of course not, Lysette!" He shouted, exasperated. "This is the most ridiculous thing; what is there to discuss? Our daughters will live and thrive safely with *us*, their *family*. End of story."

The door flew open just then. A guard addressed the prince, "your presence is requested in the great hall."

A sense of dread flooded over him, but Charles couldn't show Lysette that. Instead, he kissed his wife and his daughters before hurrying to hear the verdict.

"I love you, Lysette. No harm will come to our girls, I can promise you that."

Charles stormed into the hall, robes fanning out behind him like the wings of an eagle on the hunt. His sapphire eyes flashed between the faces in the room; his mother sitting by the fire, tightly grasping her steaming cup of tea, and his father—his King—staring blankly into the space in front of him. Movement in the far corner near the bookshelf drew his eyes to the Fae Queen and two of her guards.

Charles attempted, poorly, to keep the shock off of his face after realizing that his parents had summoned the Faeries before they had called for him. This did not bode well; it told him a decision had already been made—and without his input!

"Tell me you've put an end to this ridiculousness." Charles demanded, ignoring the satisfied, icy gaze of the Fae Queen.

King Phillip's voice was soft and slow, "no harm will come to either of the princesses."

Charles scoffed impatiently, running his hands raggedly through his auburn hair, "of course no harm will come to my children, especially—"

Phillip lifted a tired hand, silencing his son. "However, in order to prevent the fulfillment of the prophecy we have made a decision that will benefit everyone here," The King took a deep breath before continuing, "one of the princesses must leave Lark's Valley and take up residence in the non-magical realm."

"Absolutely not!" Prince Charles took an angry step forward. "Mother," he begged, turning toward the woman who always took his side, "how can you do this to me?"

The Queen stood to make her way over to her son. She brought her hand softly to his cheek, tears filling her eyes as she tried to remain strong. He softened under his mother's loving touch, smelling her favorite lavender perfume.

"Darling, don't worry," she said, "I've insisted that no member of our family will be raised by anyone other than one of our own," she exhaled a shaky breath, "I will be going with her."

Shock rendered him speechless. He sputtered for a moment before he found his voice again.

"Though I can't see how this can get much worse, why do I feel that there is more to this ever-growing nightmare than you're telling me?" Charles asked slowly.

The Fae Queen spoke then, as blunt and cold as always, "neither the Queen nor the Princess can ever return to us. They can not use their magical abilities while in the other realm, and your daughter can never know who she was or where she came from."

Charles gaped in horror, raising his voice to his father once again, "there must be another option!"

The King snapped to attention then, his booming voice filling the hall. "Enough! It has been decided. We will have to make the best of this situation and move forward—we must. For the sake of our kingdom and for the sake of our world." His voice softened for a moment, "let us treasure the time we have left with our loved ones. Go to your daughters, Charles." He addressed the rest of the room, "I need time with my wife. Leave us."

As the large doors closed behind him, the sound of his mother's sobs nearly ripped Charles's heart from his chest. Though, he knew the cries of his own wife would haunt him forever once she learned of their future.

~ One ~

OCTOBER 2014

The first few lonely snowflakes of late autumn fluttered to the ground while the front door shut behind her friend. She was alone now, more alone than she'd ever been; whether this was good or not was still up for debate.

Her grandmother's home was quite large—no, this wasn't her grandmother's house anymore; she had inherited everything just as her grandmother had wanted—but being here alone, protected by these familiar walls, was never lonely.

Remnants of her grandmother's love and warmth were still everywhere—and why wouldn't they be? Her grandmother, Charlotte, had only passed away a few days ago and Cassidy had no intentions of getting rid of any of her grandmother's things.

Cassie had never known any other family besides her grandma and with no other known relatives, she was forced to deal with this grief alone. Well, not completely alone.

Emily, her best friend since childhood, had been extremely supportive. She had been staying with Cassie to make sure she was okay, and had offered to stay another night but Cassie told her to go home. Although Cassidy loved and appreciated her best friend very much, three whole days with her had been more than enough for a while. Besides, Cassidy felt the need for a good, long crying session without an audience.

Cassie made her way over to the large picture window in the living room and took a moment to watch the falling snowflakes. Snow in late October wasn't uncommon in Northern Michigan, but Cassie knew it wouldn't accumulate. Proving her right, each delicate flake promptly melted as it touched the ground.

She felt as though she could relate; she was fading away as well. She tried so hard to feel any other emotion besides sadness and emptiness, but it just wouldn't happen.

The grief was all consuming, like a dense shadow covering everything around her, preventing her from seeing the light. Everyone continued to tell her that this would pass. It was simply going to take time. But how much time, Cassie wondered, would it take for her to convince herself that she was okay with being utterly alone?

Gone. Alone. Empty. The words kept cycling in her head, growing louder with each round. She tried to focus on her surroundings, hoping that would help block out the harsh voices. The faint sound of the wind howling outside was something worth focusing on. Cassie concentrated, imaging her sadness as a tangible thing being blown far away by the wintry gale.

She felt the cold glass on her cheek as she pressed against the window, noticing the moonlight shimmering off of the wet ground. The ghost of a smile played on the corners of Cassie's lips. It was gone as soon as it appeared, chased away by tears as she remembered what her grandma had always told her about the shimmer of the snow.

After the first snowfall during the year Cassie had started kindergarten, she and her grandma had gone outside to shovel a path. In

awe, little Cassidy had stopped just a few steps outside of the doorway.

"Grammy!" She had exclaimed, "look! Look how sparkly it is!"

Charlotte had smiled warmly down at her granddaughter—her
pride and joy—"yes, Cassie, dear. The Faeries were hard at work last
night. And look at what a wonderful job they did covering the snow
with their Faerie dust!"

Now, nearly thirteen years later, Cassie was left to admire the
snowflakes alone. The magic of the Faeries was long gone, laid to rest
along with the melting flakes and Grandma Charlotte.

Her focus shifted from the scene outside to her own reflection in
the glass. Her round, blue eyes were swollen and red from crying. She
reached up to smooth out the mess of her thin, auburn hair; hadn't
she brushed it today?

The warm tears of grief began to flow freely as Cassie sank into
her grandma's rocking chair and, eventually, fell asleep with
thoughts of Faeries consuming her dreams.

* * *

She felt as though she didn't truly wake up until months later in
June of the following year, when the snow had been melted for a little while, replaced by budding trees and green grass. She had drug
herself through the winter like a machine—sticking to routine and
only carrying out essential tasks. But winter was over now, and she
vowed to face this new season with a new outlook.

Cassie eagerly opened all of the windows in her old, two-story
home, ready to let in the warm spring breeze, hoping to flush out all
of the stale, dry air. Not only had the past few months felt like some
of the longest months of her life, but they had also been some of the
most difficult months. Thankfully, she was given as much time off of
work as she needed by her employers at the local bakery.

She requested a few more days off this week to tidy up more of her grandma's loose ends and she was glad that she did; it was a beautiful day. The flowers were budding and the forest was getting greener. This had always been her grandma's favorite time of year.

"There is just so much magic in the world during the springtime." Charlotte would say. "This is the season of new life and fresh starts. Those are two of the best things in the world."

Everything was bringing tears to Cassie's eyes these past few months and the beauty of spring was no exception. Normally, she'd rejoice for the warmer weather and greenery, but today it was just a reminder that her grandmother wouldn't get to experience her favorite season this year or any year to follow. Cassie sniffed and wiped the tears from her eyes; she had a lot to get done today and there was no room for crying in the schedule.

Grandma Charlotte requested that all of her clothing be donated to the local thrift store, but other than that, Cassie was given the option to keep anything else she wanted or donate the rest. There was no other family to distribute belongings to.

Cassie had only ever known her grandma. Never a grandfather, parents, aunts, uncles, cousins or siblings. Of course, as she was growing up she naturally questioned her lack of relatives to which Grandma Charlotte's answer was consistently: "you and I, Cassie, we will always have each other and that is all we need."

Cassie's curiosity had dwindled over the years and eventually she stopped asking about her family—or lack thereof. She couldn't say she didn't think about their absence from time to time. However, she had never felt lonely or unloved with her grandma. Her life was filled with nothing but happiness and affection.

Now, as she loaded the last of the boxes into the back of her car and closed the trunk, the only thing on her mind was how alone she truly was and yet how very loved she still felt.

Leaning against the back of the car, Cassie sighed and took a moment to look at the house—her house—that she grew up in. She had always loved it's old Victorian features and covered front porch where two rocking chairs sat. Seven sizable windows on the front of the home and several more on the sides and back let so much natural light in. The newly updated sunny-yellow siding paired perfectly with the dark brown roof and front door.

As soon as you walked in, a wide staircase led to the five bedrooms and two bathrooms on the upper level while the rest of the living space was nestled comfortably on the main floor.

Perhaps her favorite part of the house was the ten acres of forest surrounding it that she had inherited as well. As a child, she would spend hours exploring the property with her grandma, learning all about the magical creatures that Charlotte said lived in the woods: the Faeries, the Elves, the Water Sprites in the ponds and so much more. Of course, she knew now that her grandma was never being serious; she had only wanted to brighten a little girl's view on the world around her.

Granted, the house and the land it sat on might have been a bit too big for one young woman, but it was charming, perfect, and it was all hers. Besides, she wanted a family someday—a husband, maybe a few kids—and being as she grew up here, she had a first hand account of just how great of a home this was for raising a family. Nevertheless, she'd give it all up in a heartbeat if it would bring her grandma back.

Cassie took her place in the driver's seat, tossed her bag to the back where her grandmother's purse and keychain sat. Cassie's first stop was going to be the thrift store, but then she had to finish taking care of her grandma's things at the bank and some other random places. She was saving the worst project for last: trying to figure out what all of the keys on the key chain were for.

She had already determined which were the house keys and her grandma's car keys. Cassie was fairly certain that there was a storage unit key, a safe box key, and a post office box key among the mess as well. There were still a few keys, though, that she had no idea what they unlocked.

Charlotte was always keeping Cassie on her toes with riddles and puzzles. It seemed like this might be the last one that Cassie had left to solve.

* * *

Later that night, Cassie sat slumped at the kitchen table with all of her grandma's keys spread out in front of her. She was simply staring at the pile of metal on the table, hoping for the answer to just jump out at her. Cassie had called in reinforcements (her best friend, Emily) and together they were going to solve this puzzle.

Just then, Cassie heard a car door slam shut in the driveway. Emily knew she was welcome and didn't knock before coming in the front door.

"Cassie?" Emily's voice echoed through the house.

"In here, Emmy!" Cassie called back.

"Okay," Emily chirped as she rounded the corner, "what's the crisis?" Her eyes moved to the pile of keys on the table. "Jeez, Cassie, did you murder a janitor or something? Where did you get all of these keys?"

Cassie scoffed, "these are my grandma's keys. I'm trying to figure out what they all go to." She began taking individual keys and separating them from the pile, naming off their uses as she went. She continued to remove the known keys from the unknown keys until there were only three left.

"I cannot think of what these three go to and that's what I need your help with."

"Well," Emily sighed, twirling a perfectly polished blonde lock of hair around her finger, "I could think of many more glamorous ways to spend my Friday evening, but we might as well get started." She scooped up the three remaining keys and off they went.

"Did Charlotte have any locking drawers in her study?" Emily asked.

"Checked that already. There was a lock on the desk drawer but nothing else in that room."

"What about her bedroom?"

Cassie hesitated. She had only been in her grandma's room once since she passed and that was just a quick in-and-out endeavor for the sole purpose of gathering clothes for donation. Cassie didn't want to go through her grandma's more personal items just yet. She knew it had almost been eight months, but as long as her room remained untouched, it was almost as if she were still here.

"I haven't really looked around in there yet." She admitted.

"Do you want me to?" Emily asked quietly, her brown eyes soft with concern.

Cassie nodded.

"I'll be right back."

Emily was only in the room for a few moments before returning hold out the smallest key.

"This one unlocks the jewelry box. One mystery solved, two more to go!" She smiled her bright, beauty queen smile.

After combing through every room in the house twice, their search led them outside and into the shed where they discovered one of the keys was to her grandmother's old riding lawn mower.

"Really, Cassie?" Emily had sighed. "Your first thought wasn't to check all of the machinery?"

"Well, I checked her car..." Cassie pouted. "Besides, this old hunk of junk hasn't been used in years. I'm surprised it still starts. Gram would hire neighborhood boys to mow the lawn. She said it kept them out of trouble, but really they just spent the money on bad things anyways."

Cassie chuckled at the memory: watching her grandma pay the boys a few bucks and then seeing them later on trying to get their older brothers to buy them cigarettes or booze. Grandma Charlotte was a wise and brilliant woman but sometimes she forgot how mischievous young children could be. Cassie couldn't count the number of times that she'd snuck out to hang out with Emily on school nights!

With only one key left the girls continued their search for the final lock. For hours they scoured through the shed, the garage, and the house with no luck. Finally, as a last resort they decided to search the internet; maybe a detailed description of the key in the browser would give them some kind of lead.

Emily's dainty fingers flew across the keyboard and then hit send. The results were back in less than a second. "Sorry, Cassie. All that popped up were ads to purchase novelty keys and other junk."

"It would help if there was a brand name or serial number or something on this key." Cassie muttered.

"Cassie, I think we should just call it a night and accept that this key is just for decoration." Emily closed the laptop. "We should order dinner and stay in tonight, watch some movies and have a girl's night. What do you say?"

Cassie smiled sadly and nodded in agreement. "I think I'm just more upset about not being able to simply ask her myself, you know?" Tears stung her eyes, "I don't really care about whatever it is that this key unlocks, I just want to be able to talk to her about this—about anything really."

"I know." Emily wrapped her arms around her best friend, "I understand."

~ Two ~

Three hours and two orders of Chinese take-out later, Emily and Cassie were in bed asleep. Cassie had put the key on a simple gold chain that Grandma Charlotte had gotten her for her birthday a few years ago. She had fallen asleep clutching the mystery key and, for the first time since her death, Grandma Charlotte appeared in Cassie's dreams.

Cassie knew she was dreaming but she wasn't anywhere fantastical; she was on the floor, sitting next to the fireplace in her living room. The room was dark and the only light came from the flames that danced in the hearth, the shadows jumped around the room to the same crackling beat.

In this dream, it was the middle of winter. Outside, the long limbs of the pine trees hung low as they attempted to support the wet, heavy snow that had settled on top of them. The snow was still falling gently outside and everything glistened in the light of the full moon.

Something moved in her peripheral vision, startling her. She spun around only to see that there was someone sitting in Grandma Charlotte's rocking chair.

"Grammy?" Cassie's voice cracked as she saw her grandmother's familiar, thin silhouette in the old chair.

Charlotte smiled and stood slowly before taking a step towards her granddaughter but Cassie was already bounding across the room to embrace her grandma.

"Oh, Cassie, sweetheart." Charlotte said, smoothing the hair on Cassie's head as she sobbed. "We don't have much time together, who knows when you'll wake up from this dream? Let's not spend this time crying."

Cassie knew she was right, but this dream was so realistic it was hard not to cry. Cassie hugged her grandma a little tighter, inhaling a bit more of her familiar lavender perfume before pulling away and drying her eyes.

"Is this really you? Or am I just imagining you as part of my grief?" Cassie fought back more tears.

Charlotte chuckled sadly, "I'm as real as you want me to be."

"You'll never be that real, Grandma. If it were up to me I'd be hugging you in person, not in a dream."

"Well, in any case, I wanted to tell you how proud I am of you. You've been so brave and strong throughout your life and especially lately."

Cassie sniffled, "I feel so alone. You're all the family I've had my whole life, and all the family I will ever have. What do I do now, without you?"

Charlotte held her at arm's length. "Cassidy, you move forward—no, you *march* forward. Be brave and strong like I know you are. Be cautious and wise as I know you know how to be. Be as thoughtful and understanding as you can be because soon, Cassie, everything you know and believe in is going to be challenged."

Still overwhelmed by her emotions, Cassie struggled to process what her grandmother was saying. "Gram, I don't understand."

"I know you've already looked in my study, but look again. Your answer is in my literature. I've had to keep you hidden from the truth for so long, but now it's time that you know. The lock that you've been looking for... it's there among the books."

The dream began to fray at the edges; consciousness was pulling at Cassie's mind, trying to bring her back to reality. She fought like a fish on a hook.

"I don't want to wake up, Grammy, please, stay with me!"

Charlotte wrapped Cassie in a tight hug, "this isn't goodbye forever, just for now. I love you, Cassidy."

Before Cassie could say the four little words *I love you too*, she was awake. The warmth of her grandma's hug was just a ghost on her skin. She stared up at the dark ceiling of her bedroom with a heavy feeling in her heart.

Emily was still sleeping peacefully, her long blonde hair spread out on the pillow under her head. Cassie stretched her stiff muscles—falling asleep in your day clothes was never very comfy. She looked over at her friend and sighed, knowing she wasn't going to fall back asleep anytime soon. Instead of waking Emily up Cassie decided to roll out of bed.

The red lights of her alarm clock screamed one o'clock in the morning and from behind fluffy clouds, faint traces of moonlight brightened the sky outside her window. Cassie only admired the calm scene for a moment before she knew what she had to do. It might have been a dream, but Grandma Charlotte told her to recheck the study and that's what she was going to do.

Cassie quietly opened the door and slipped out into the hallway leaving Emily to snore softly alone. She latched the door behind her soundlessly and expertly dodged all of the creaky floor boards on her way to the study. Charlotte had been a light sleeper and in order for Cassie to sneak out of her bedroom it had been essential that she learn which parts of the floor would groan when stepped on.

It took Cassie's complete focus to not look at her grandmother's door as she passed it, knowing she would be tempted to go inside and never come out. Right now she was on a mission and couldn't afford distractions.

Cassie felt a little silly sneaking around her own house. She just couldn't ignore the instinct telling her there was a need to be careful, though she couldn't guess why she had that feeling at all. She picked up her pace as she entered the spacious study and closed the door behind her.

In the curved room a writing desk sat in front of a large round window looking out at the forest. Bookshelves were built into the eastern and western walls from floor to ceiling and they were jam-packed with books.

Some of the books were so old that Cassie had never been allowed to touch them for fear of damaging the pages and others were brand new tombs filled with modern knowledge. In any case, Cassie knew she would have a lot of work to do looking through everything.

She pulled out a few books from the eye level shelf of the book-case to her left. These were some of the particularly old ones, so she gently set them on the desk and took a seat. By the time Cassie was finished skimming through the pages of each book in front of her, an hour or so had passed and the moon had made its way out from be-hind the clouds, its light fully illuminating the room around her.

Having found no useful information—just pointless facts about the geography of countries that didn't even exist anymore, and me-dieval medical practices—she sighed and heaved the books back into their resting places on the shelves.

Reluctantly, she started gathering another arm full of books. As she grabbed the last book she could carry, her hand brushed against something smooth and cold on the back of the book case. Cassie quickly and gently set her heavy pile of books on the desk and went back to investigate.

Carved into the dark wood was what Cassie could only describe as a keyhole. The sides of the dusty keyhole were outlined with gold paint that shimmered in the silver moonlight. Before she even realized what she was doing, the old key was in her hand and Cassie was inserting it into the lock.

Slowly, the key reached the end of the hole; it was a perfect fit. After she turned it clockwise just a quarter of the way, Cassie released the breath she hadn't known she was holding and jumped back, the key securely on the chain around her neck.

Slowly, the bookshelf began to come away from the wall behind it. Dust filled the study as the secret door revealed a dark, rounded opening in the wall. The corridor walls were covered in thick, rough-cut stone with no light to brighten the path. A smooth staircase descended into darkness while a cold, musty draft brushed across Cassie's face.

"What..." she muttered to herself, trying to figure out where on earth this staircase could possibly lead to.

Cassie had grown up in this old house thinking she knew every nook and cranny, but apparently she was wrong; there was one more place left to discover.

She scurried over to the desk. After rummaging through the drawers for a moment she finally found what she was looking for; a small flashlight. With a click of the button, a beam of light cut through the dust floating in the air around the passageway.

Her first step onto the cold stone stairs sent shivers up her spine. For a moment she considered going back to get Emily, but part of her wondered if she was still dreaming; in which case, she decided, she would be perfectly fine on her own.

In the end, her curiosity was stronger than her worry, and she cautiously pressed onward.

In the stairwell, which had become home to a variety of spiders and other insects, the air was stagnant and dry. Cassie did her best to avoid the cobwebs and creepy-crawlies but despite her best efforts she still ended up with a few old webs in her hair.

As she approached the end of the stairs, a faint light came from whatever lay at the bottom. The light grew brighter and her wonder grew stronger the further she descended. Cassie was relieved when she finally reached the source: a heavy-looking, rounded, wooden door with moonlight and crisp night air seeping through the cracks.

Now, Cassie was really confused. There were only two exterior doors on this old house—one in the front and one on the side by the kitchen—plus, she had walked so far down that, reasonably, she should be underground. So, how could there possibly be light and fresh air behind this door?

Slowly, she pushed open the door and found herself in her familiar backyard. Cassie stepped out onto the dew-covered lawn and sighed.

Well, that was anticlimactic, she thought.

She turned around to head back through the door she had just come out of, and her heart skipped a beat.

Directly behind her was a building that was eerily similar to her house, but it certainly wasn't her house—it couldn't be. The door to the passageway had vanished; only the rough wood exterior of the house remained. This wood, however, was not painted a happy pale yellow, like her home was. What she saw in front of her was old and chipped with only a few yellow paint flecks stuck to its weathered surface. Her gaze shifted upward to the rusty metal roof when a bit of movement caught her eye; a sheer white curtain was gently blowing out of one of the shattered upstairs windows.

Another shiver ran up her spine but this time it wasn't from the cold. Cassie decided for certain she must still be dreaming; there was no other explanation for how weird things were getting.

Cautiously, she crept around the house. This house had exactly the same structure as her home—all windows and doors in the same place as well as the same length and height of all of the walls—but this building sitting in front of her had to be at least a hundred years older and much less cared for.

Cassie made her way up the broken front steps and into the house through the gaping hole where the front door was supposed to be. Dead leaves were strewn everywhere inside and a few rogue plants had pushed their way up through the floorboards. Another huge hole had opened up in the roof in the middle of the foyer, letting in the rain and sunlight that these little plants needed to survive.

Things were getting creepier by the minute as Cassie quickly realized that the interior of this house was a spitting image of her home as well. Everything from the furniture to the decor in the house was destroyed, of course; ruined either by the elements, vandals or animals.

Watching her step very carefully for fear of falling through the rotted floor, she took herself to the upper level of the house. If this house was identical to hers, then maybe there would be another secret passage to travel back through to get home.

Unsurprisingly, the study was right were she thought it would be. Cassie jumped over a hole in the floor to to get into the room where, much to her relief, she found the same book case with the same keyhole. Cassie inserted then turned the key and ran down the stairs after the bookcase moved out of the way as she had hoped it would.

Her logic continued to prove to be correct: at the end of the stairs was the same wooden door she had passed through the first time. Cassie wasted no time exiting the passageway and after the did, she found herself in her real backyard. She wasn't even completely shocked when she turned to find the door was gone once again.

"Okay," she said aloud to herself, "time to wake up from this extremely strange dream."

Cassie concentrated on waking up with all of her might. The problem was that she didn't feel like she was asleep; she felt completely lucid and conscious. Cassie pinched and slapped herself—which actually hurt—and rolled around in the cold, wet grass with no success. As she stood up, chilly and damp, she heard a window sliding open above her.

"Cassie?" Emily was leaning out of Cassie's bedroom window. "What the hell are you doing?"

"Um... Dreaming?" Cassie responded.

Emily stared down at her incredulously. "Are you having a nervous breakdown or something? Do I need to call someone? Come inside!"

Cassie's heart was pounding so hard that her vision shook as she made her way back inside. Had she really been awake the whole time?

Emily met her at the front door. "For real, Cassie, what were you doing in the backyard?"

"Emmy," Cassie looked her directly in the eyes, "if I'm not dreaming—if I'm *really* awake right now—something crazy is happening."

Emily let out a small, nervous sound, "Cassie, you're kinda freaking me out."

"I'm freaking out too!" Cassie shouted. "Come on, we have to check on something."

~ Three ~

Emily warily let Cassie lead her up the stairs and into the study. As they rounded the corner, Cassie wasn't sure what she'd rather deal with: not finding the hidden staircase and just accepting that she was crazy, or finding the staircase and having to accept that she was dealing with something beyond her understanding.

Cassie's heart fluttered a bit with relief—and a bit with fear, too—upon entering the study. The bookcase was still displaced and where it had sat was the same hole-in-the-wall stairwell.

"What is this, Cassie?" Emily stood at the top of the stone staircase and peered down into the darkness.

"I had a dream where Grandma told me that the old key would unlock something here in the study." Cassie pointed to the stairwell. "This is what it opened."

"Okay," Emily looked over at Cassie, "but where does it go? And, this still doesn't explain what you were doing in the backyard."

Cassie sighed, pulled out her flashlight, then headed down the stairs. When Emily didn't immediately follow, Cassie looked over her shoulder.

"Are you coming?" she asked.

Emily couldn't seem to get the disbelieving look off of her face and Cassie couldn't blame her—Cassie couldn't believe she was keeping it together as well as she was—but Emily still followed her best friend.

After they both fully entered the corridor, the bookshelf creaked shut behind them. Cassie was extra thankful for her flashlight; without it they would have been in total darkness.

The girls' shoes slapped against the stone steps on the way down. Emily squealed occasionally when she got too close to insects and their webs. Cassie chuckled quietly; even in the strangest of situations she could always count on Emily to be the same, squeamish girl she'd always been.

When they reached the wooden door, Cassie took a deep breath. She turned to look at her friend.

"When we walk through here you have to promise me you won't totally lose it."

Emily crossed her arms, "I'm not promising anything, but please open the door so that we can get away from these bugs!"

Cassie pushed the door open, muttering, "bugs are the least of our problems."

They had only just emerged in the yard when Emily threw her hands up in frustration. "Enough with the games, Cassie, what's so weird about being in your backyard?"

Cassie took her friend by the shoulders and gently turned her to face the abandoned house behind them. "This isn't my backyard."

"What..." Emily stared open-mouthed at the old building. "How? Where... Cassie?"

Cassie shook her head, "I have no idea what's going on here, all that I know is that Grandma must have wanted me to find this."

"So, let's assume that the dream you had wasn't just a dream and your grandma actually visited you from beyond the grave. She told you how to find the door which led us here. Did she say anything else? Like, where *here* is?"

"All that she said was that it was time I learn the truth."

Emily scoffed, "well, what do we do now? Have you already been inside?"

Cassie nodded. "Yeah, but only for a second. Maybe we could go in together?"

"Yeah, we should."

They wandered around inside the old house in silence until Emily finally spoke up. "So this is exactly the same as your house, your grandma knew about it and wanted you to find it, but she didn't tell you why or what this is. A vision of the future, maybe?" Emily guessed. "Everything here seems really old."

Suddenly Cassie had an idea. "If this is the same house, then maybe Grandma's room is the same too. Let's see if we can find something in there."

Cassie tried to sound hopeful, but when you had no idea what exactly you were searching for, there was a good chance it would be impossible to find.

The girls rushed upstairs and into what they believed would be Charlotte's room. Sure enough, they were right. While the decor was a little dated, everything else was essentially the same and this room appeared to be mostly untouched by vandals or other destructive elements.

The drawers and doors of each dresser and closet were wide open and the contents were missing. Scraps of clothing that had been left behind were strewn across the room and the jewelry box had been emptied and knocked to the ground.

"Look, Cassie." Emily was standing next to the bed. She lifted a broken picture frame from the night stand.

Emily gently took the photo out from behind the shattered glass and flipped it over, reading the spidery handwriting on the back. "'Larken Family, 1996. From the left, Queen Charlotte, King Phillip,

Prince Charles, and Princess Lysette, at the cabin on the hill,'" Emily stopped for a moment. "Cassie, this... it looks like you have more family out there."

After a moment of awkward silence Cassie snatched the photo from her friend's hand. She sat on the old, tattered bed and stared at it for a long while. Obviously, Cassie couldn't know for sure, but it looked conceivable that this may in fact be a portrait of the family Cassie never knew she had.

Family. Something she had craved all her life, and here they were smiling in an old, yellowed photograph. The old ghost of hope she used to have for finding her family began to awaken after a decade long slumber. Cassie forced the useless emotion away, attempting to keep her cool.

"Well, they didn't care enough to come find me," she said, bitterly.

The photograph appeared to be taken in front of the home, back when it was in much better condition. Standing proudly on the lawn was a man, tall and muscular with striking blue eyes and a full, thick head of hair. Next to him, glowing with joy and cradling her pregnant belly, was a slender woman whose head only came up to her husband's shoulder. In front of these parents sat an older couple, enjoying a picnic on a white and red plaid blanket.

Her grandmother was not only recognizable but radiant and nearly eighteen years younger, in an expensive-looking tea-length gown. In fact, everyone looked extravagant. The man standing next to her grandmother, Phillip—her grandfather possibly?—was dressed in tailored clothes and the same was true for the younger man and woman—Charles and Lysette.

The attire, though, that stood out the most was not the clothes on their backs, but the crowns on their heads. The older gentleman,

Phillip, wore the largest crown, a massive piece nearly the size of his own head. The crowns grew smaller from Charlotte's to Charles's and, finally, Lysette's tiara.

It didn't take long for Cassie to recognize the similarities between herself and the young couple in the photo. So these were her parents. They sure seemed happy for two people about to abandon their baby. How did they choose? Cassie wondered. She studied the woman's face. Did this mother really give up her child or chose one over the other?

"What do you want to do now?" Emily whispered.

Cassie took a deep breath before responding. "I don't know what's going on here, but I can't just leave now. I trust Grandma Charlotte completely. Whatever all of this is," she waved the photo in the air and gestured to the room around her, "she knew I would come here. She wanted me to. I understand if you want to go home," Cassie sighed, "but I have to see this through. What if these people are still here? What if they are why my grandmother led me here?"

"I can't leave you here alone." Emily smiled and let out a listless chuckle, "if I went back now, there's no way I could just carry on with a normal day and forget about all of this."

Cassie refrained from asking the first question that popped into her frustrated mind: *and you think you're going to be of much help to me?* Instead she decided to go another direction: perhaps appealing to Emily's personal sense of safety would sway her to head back and let Cassie deal with this on her own.

"What about your family? The salon you want to open in the future? If things are as crazy as they seem here, it could be dangerous. I can't ask you to come with me."

"Well, you didn't ask me to do anything." Emily stood tall, one hand on her hip, "I'm here because I want to be and I'm staying because I want to. You can't stop me."

Cassie sighed. She had seen that stubborn look on Emily's face enough times to know that no matter what was said from here on out, Emily's mind was made up. Maybe it would be nice to have a familiar face around.

"Emily Jane, you're so stubborn."

Side by side they then made their way outside. As they took their first step out onto the front lawn, Emily's stomach gurgled.

"If this world is a mirror of ours," Emily smiled sheepishly, "then maybe the amazing cafe in town could be our first stop?"

Cassie rolled her eyes. "Emmy, we aren't here as tourists. We have to find my family. Plus, it's so late at night, I doubt anything is open."

Emily's stomach rumbled again, "okay but, hear me out. Your grandma didn't leave a map or anything and there's no use starving ourselves. Plus, maybe there's someone who can give us directions!"

Cassie was about to object when her own stomach gurgled. "Alright," she said, "fine. But if anything is even open, we are only stopping for something quick to eat."

Pleased with her successful persuasion, Emily smiled and started walking down the driveway with Cassie following closely behind.

"Cassie, I gotta tell ya, I really didn't think my weekend was going to be anywhere *near* this interesting when I came over earlier. But, jeez! Me? What about you! I mean, how bizarre is all of this? Like..."

Cassie began to tune out the chatter; she had enough to think about.

Bizarre, Emily had said. That didn't begin to cover it. How about: confusing or terrifying or heartbreaking? Cassie had thought that holding on to the memory of her grandma might bring her joy or give her a cute, innocent story to tell her children one day. The last thing she would've expected was another world and a secret family.

Cassidy trusted and loved her grandmother more than anything but so many questions and doubts flooded her mind. First and foremost: why? Why did her grandma hide so much from her? And, why, *oh why*, couldn't Grandma Charlotte have had a conversation about all of this before she died?

Cassie's train of thought derailed for a moment then, and she started to focus on what Emily was saying.

"Things don't seem too crazy around here just yet. I wonder what we'll find when we get to town." Emily mused.

"I'm not sure I even want to think about it. Maybe we'll get lucky and it's not too unlike what what we're used to. I don't think I have the mental capacity to handle any more surprises today."

Then, in a remarkable turn of events, the girls walked in silence; not even Chatterbox Emily had anything to say. Cassie welcomed the peace and enjoyed the simple sound of gravel under their shoes.

After a short while, the two of them rounded the final corner and found themselves at the top of a massive hill overlooking the small town nestled in the valley.

The light of the full moon clearly illuminated the view below, casting a silvery blanket across the entire valley. A few lights in the town twinkled in the darkness, mimicking the stars in the night sky. So far, everything looked similar to the town they grew up in—the same hills and the same river cutting through the familiar valley—except for a few differences, one most noticeable of all.

"Is that a castle?" Emily pointed straight ahead.

On the other side of the town, atop the other large hill that rose up on the opposite side of the valley, sat a rather monumental structure.

"It's hard to tell from here, but it certainly looks important with that huge wall surrounding it." If Cassie squinted and focused, she could almost make out flags flying on and around the building.

They continued toward the town, and with every step the butter-flies in Cassie's stomach fluttered faster and harder. As the first few buildings came into view, Cassie couldn't seem to will her feet to take her one more step forward.

"Cassie?" Emily's face housed a look of concern. "You okay?"

Cassie could only manage a whisper while staring wide-eyed at the short distance separating them from the town, "I don't think I can do this."

Emily took a step toward Cassie, "do you want to turn back?"

Slowly, Cassie looked at her friend. "I know I have nothing waiting for me back there. I'm just afraid of what might be waiting for me in there." Her eyes shifted back toward the town.

Emily grabbed her hand and tugged lightly, "well, we aren't going to find out by just standing here, are we?" Cassie shook her head and Emily smiled. "Then let's be brave."

Cassie nodded silently and continued forward with her grandma's words echoing in her mind. *Be brave and strong like I know you are*, Charlotte had said. The love of her grandmother seemed to physi-cally warm her heart giving Cassie the strength to stroll right into the valley town with her head held high.

As they crossed the threshold of the town where the dirt gradu-ally became cobblestone, a large fountain rose up in the middle of the path. The copper that probably once glistened in the sunlight, was now dull and turning green as the water flowed across the sculpture. The focal point of the fountain was a carving of a bird in flight, face pointed toward the sky with the main flow of water coming from its open beak.

The water was coming out in just a slight trickle and one of the wings was chipped and bent while the other was nearly completely broken off. This once magnificent piece of art was now clearly for-gotten and not at all cared for.

Emily read the crooked plaque posted on the bird's chest, "this statue erected in honor of King Jeremiah Larken, the Bringer of Peace. Long live the Larken family."

The girls exchanged a wide eyed look. It took Cassie a moment before being able to speak again.

"It's just a total coincidence that this King and I have the same last name and everyone in that family photo was wearing a crown. Right?"

"Sure. *Coincidence.*" Emily rolled her eyes. "Should I start calling you princess?" Emily giggled.

Cassie laughed and punched her friend gently in the arm, "please, never call me that. This proves nothing. It could just be a common last name around here. That's all."

Emily threw up her hands and took a step backwards, as if claiming innocence, "okay, I won't call you that, I promise." Cassie knew by the smirk on her friend's face that it was a lie, but she let it slide. "But can we talk about the possibility that you might just be royalty?"

"If this dilapidated statue is any indication of how this place treats their royalty, I don't think I want to be part of that."

"What are you doing out after curfew?" A gruff voice called out. Cassie jumped; she hadn't even heard anyone walk up behind them.

They spun around meeting a tall, armored man. His silver garb looked astonishingly fitted to his body, almost like a second skin. Extremely pale skin showed here and there where there was no armor, and a pair of bright purple eyes looked down on them. If that wasn't strange enough, long, pointed ears stuck out from specially carved holes in his helmet.

Cassie spoke first, "um, so sorry sir... we're just a little lost."

The man's stance was unwavering. "Lost or not you're out after curfew. Humans need to be in their homes by midnight, no exceptions. You know the rules." He began to reach for his sword sheathed at his side.

"There you are!" Another man's voice cut through the silent night air. "Been looking everywhere for you!"

A slender boy appeared at Cassie's side, wrapping his arms around her in a tight hug, he whispered so only she could hear, "trust me," then, louder, "your trip must have taken a lot longer than expected, cousin."

The guard remained stoic. "They're with you?"

"Of course," the boy's muscular arm remained tight around Cassie's shoulders, "I've been expecting them all day. Let me escort them home," he tugged on her lightly, leading Cassie and Emily away from the soldier, "very sorry if this caused you any trouble."

The guard grunted but allowed the three of them to walk away, calling after them, "you head straight home! I will not be lenient if I find you out here again!"

"Almost there, keep walking," the boy whispered.

Cassie stayed silent, allowing him to lead them around the corner and through a tight alley. After a moment, they came out on a wide and empty street. He quickly turned right, keeping a firm hand on their lower backs guiding them forward.

As they hurried over the cobblestones, Cassie quickly noticed her first perception was wrong; this town was nothing like the one back home. There were none of the familiar shops or street names, not to mention there wasn't a single vehicle in sight. The streets were empty and the shops were dark; people really seemed to take that curfew seriously around here.

Finally, as Cassie saw the town's outer wall coming into view, she spoke up. "Hey, where are you taking us?"

"Somewhere safe." He simply replied.

Cassie looked up at him then, noticing he too had pointed ears like the soldier, but they were a normal length. Stranger than his ears was the thick mass of fire-engine-red hair piled in a tight bun atop his head. His skin, a golden, sun-tanned color, was stretched tight around defined muscles. He was on guard, looking down every alley they passed.

"Can you at least tell us your name?" Emily whispered harshly.

His eyes flashed to her for a moment before continuing to scan the streets. "Rhett." he stated.

He didn't seem much in the mood for talking, Cassie thought, but she really wanted to ask him just one more question: why did he save them? She refrained, instead glancing over at Emily who was staring back at her. They both made questioning faces but remained silent.

They soon crossed the border and exited the town. Rhett led them along the edge of the high wall and after a few more steps Cassie began to hear a *woosh, woosh, woosh* rising and falling in a perfect steady rhythm. The ground beneath them went from cobblestone to grass and finally a vast expanse of water lay a few hundred feet in front of them surrounded by a sandy beach. The black waves lapped the shoreline leaving the sand beneath them stained a darker brown.

Further down the beach, to the east, the grassy hillside extended up and jutted out, rising and ending in a cliff, the north face of which was a nearly vertical scarp. Atop the massive precipice sat a huge house-like structure; its windows dark. Was that where Rhett was taking them?

He stopped suddenly just as they reached the edge of the grass before stepping onto the beach.

"I shouldn't have assumed that you needed my help," he began, staring through narrowed eyes at them, "but you two were noticeably out of place back there. Every human in Lark's Valley knows about curfew. Tell me, what were you doing out?"

Cassie opened her mouth to respond but nothing came out, she looked to Emily for help, but she was equally as clueless. Cassie cleared her throat, trying to sound more confident than she felt.

"Well... as we told that guy back there, we really are lost. We... aren't from around here."

Rhett stood, arms crossed, face twisted in a thoughtful expression as he continued to examine them for a moment. "You sure you weren't out for the meeting?"

Cassie wasn't sure if the expression on her face looked more panicked or confused, but either way her words left her mouth before her brain had a chance to register what she was saying.

"You caught us,"she nervously chuckled.

Emily whispered an anxious, "Cassie..."

Rhett's expression softened a bit and he spun, walking in the sand towards the cliff side. "Well, we're already late." He called over his shoulder, "come on; hurry up."

As Rhett made his way through the sand, Emily grabbed Cassie's shoulder, her annoyance clear in her voice, "what are you doing? What's the plan here?"

"I have no idea what I'm doing," Cassie admitted, "but its cold, dark, and honestly kind of scary here. I figured since he helped us out back there he must be a decent person... right? Maybe we should stick with him for a bit."

The look of I-think-you're-insane never left Emily's face but instead she just sighed and went after Rhett. Cassie followed as well, picking up the pace to close the distance between them.

~ Four ~

Instead of rounding his path up to the home on the hill like Cassie thought he would, Rhett stayed on the beach, headed for the bottom of the cliff. Waves crashed high on the rocks there that stood tall and jagged, spraying the three of them in a fine, salty mist.

As they neared their destination, Rhett held his hand, palm outward, toward the rock wall at the base of the cliff side. A low rumble vibrated through the hill. Accompanying the odd sound, dust and small pebbles began to fall from the rock immediately in front of them.

At first, the pattern of the rubble seemed random, but slowly Cassie could see the ridges forming into the shape of an oval nearly as tall as she was. Suddenly, the rest of the rock and dirt fell away into a small pile at their feet revealing a passageway dug into the cliff side.

Cassie and Emily silently gaped at each other while Rhett crouched down and stepped inside. He glanced over his shoulder, a quizzical look on his face.

"Is there something on my back?" He reached a long arm around to brush his lower back. "Why do you have those looks on your faces?"

Emily gestured out in front of her, "This... you just... made the rock fall away?"

Rhett laughed as if Emily had just told the funniest joke, "oh, please, like you've never seen a Cloaked Door. It's one of the first spells everyone learns. Come on, or we'll miss the whole meeting."

"Yeah Em," Cassie teased, "it's just a Cloaked Door. Obviously."

"Oh shut up." Emily hissed quietly, "you weren't any less surprised."

Cassie chuckled and entered the cold, damp walkway behind Rhett, Emily following closely after her. As soon as Emily had completely entered, the small pile of dirt that had fallen to unveil the passage began to reform itself, sealing the entry behind them. As it did so, a few hundred brightly glowing stones embedded in the rock walls revealed themselves, casting an eerie orange glow throughout the small space.

Cassie couldn't help but hang her mouth open in amazement while she continued to follow Rhett through the hill. Soon, voices could be heard up ahead. The narrow path began to widen until they found themselves in a wide cavern. This circular space was illuminated by even brighter orange stones than the ones in the tunnel, and was filled with at least fifty or so people.

The crowd was focused on a man speaking to them from atop a large rock. Behind this man stood a thin woman and next to her a slightly shorter girl, their hands clasped neatly in front of them.

Rhett shuffled in behind the crowd, leaning up against the wall to listen to the speech. Emily ran into the back of Cassie who had stopped, rooted where she stood.

"Cassie," Emily whispered, squeezing around her friend to see what was going on, "what's wrong?" Her voice tapered off when she saw what it was that had frozen Cassie in place. "Oh. Oh, dear."

Oh dear doesn't even begin to cover it, Cassie thought, staring up at the people on the makeshift stage. More accurately, staring up at her parents and her sister. The older couple were undoubtedly the same people from the photo found at the old house. The years had been kind to Charles and Lysette, as they seemingly hadn't aged much at all.

What had shocked Cassie the most, though, was how much she looked like her sister, whom she presumed to be the girl standing next to Lysette. They were built so similarly: long legs held up a short, not thin but not fat, frame topped by a round face with high cheekbones, large eyes and thin lips. This girl was a bit more muscular, however, and held herself with a confidence Cassie had never had.

"With all of that being said, we can't deny the tremendous progress we have made!" Charles boomed and the crowd cheered. "Of course, we can not say we are anywhere near where we want to be. No, we can't stop until we have reclaimed the throne of Lark's Valley! The Fae's reign will soon come to an end, and our rebellion will be victorious."

The crowd cheered one loud, "down with the Faeries!"

Charles spoke at a normal volume, though the cavern echoed enough that Cassie had no problem hearing what he had to say, "in conclusion, we must stay strong. We must tirelessly hone our magical abilities and make the enhancement of our physical strength a priority. We know the Fae's army will not be easy to beat when the time comes and we must be masters of our game."

Lysette stepped forward. Lovingly, she rest her hand on her husband's arm as she addressed the crowd, "we know it's late, so thank you for coming to the last-minute meeting tonight. Go and be with your families. Safe travels home!"

With that, the crowd began to disperse. Cassie realized quickly that she was still standing in the middle of the exit and jumped to the side before the throng of people trampled her down. She and Emily went to stand by Rhett who seemed in no hurry to move from his spot along the wall.

"Seems we missed more of the meeting than I thought." Rhett shrugged. "No worries, I'll get a recap at breakfast tomorrow, I'm sure."

Cassie's eyes had been glued to her family, but even so, she couldn't find it in herself to react as they sauntered across the room towards where she and the others were standing. A light panic rose up the back of her neck as a million questions flooded her mind. Had they recognized her? Of course not, they had never seen her before. Perhaps they suspected that she didn't belong there. Was it as obvious as it felt?

"Rhett," Lysette sounded disappointed, "it's unlike you to be so late. Was something the matter?"

Rhett removed himself from the wall and bent at the waist, bowing before Lysette and Charles. "I apologize. I was in town making sure no one was having trouble sneaking out when I found these two being questioned by a Fae soldier." Rhett nodded in their direction and suddenly all eyes were on them.

Cassie could immediately feel herself begin to blush, a response to nervousness she had always experienced and had always hated. She moved to hide behind Emily a bit, who smiled brightly and bowed as Rhett had, elbowing Cassie and encouraging her to do the same. She obliged as Emily spoke.

"I am Emily Williams and this is Cassidy L—" she cleared her throat when Cassie poked her from behind, "Cassie Logan."

"Miss Logan," Lysette took a step forward, "are you alright? You look a tad bewildered."

Cassie swallowed hard, had she been staring too much? "I'm just tired. Emily and I have traveled a long way." *A very long way,* she thought.

"Then you must lodge with us! Any supporter of our cause is welcome in our home," Charles loudly proclaimed, "Miss Williams, Miss Logan, I insist."

Cassie looked to her right at Rhett who seemed as shocked as she felt, then to her left at Emily whose excitement was clear.

"I—" Cassie stammered, "that would be great, thank you."

"Wonderful," Charles smiled brightly before turning to Rhett, "Mr. Daniels, I'll catch you up on what you missed while Lysette and Divina help our guests get settled in." The two of them headed off toward the exit leaving Cassie and Emily alone with Lysette and Divina.

"After you," Lysette motioned towards the exit. Divina was the first to silently take her leave, Emily and Cassie followed with Lysette bringing up the rear.

Not a word was said as the four of them made their way through the orange cavern. Cassie couldn't seem to calm the panic rising in her throat. This was all too much; she and Emily should have just went home, moved the bookshelf back where it belonged and talked all of this up to some crazy dream.

She sighed inwardly, knowing they had come too far for that now. She focused on taking deep breaths to calm herself while Divina opened the Cloaked Door at the end of the path just the same as Rhett had.

They all filed out onto the beach, the cool night air filling their lungs. Cassie could see Rhett and Charles up ahead; Charles was talking loudly, throwing his hands all around to better describe whatever it was he was saying.

It was Lysette who broke their group's silence then as they rounded the corner and made their way up the grassy hill.

"Are you being expected elsewhere, girls? Should we send word to whomever you're staying with so that they don't worry?"

"We weren't exactly prepared for our visit," Cassie admitted truthfully, followed by a lie, "we were hoping to find lodging in town."

"Well you weren't going to find anything there," Divina spoke for the first time, looking wistfully towards the quiet little valley town, "the Fae Queen," she sneered at the word, "had the inns all shut down, and those that refused to close got burned to the ground."

"Why?" Emily asked, shocked.

"She isn't fond of outsiders," Lysette explained, "she thought by taking away the hospitalities it would discourage tourists. I'm surprised you two were allowed in at all. That Fae guard you ran into must have been in a good mood."

Cassie recalled the Fae man's glare. If that was him in good spirits, she couldn't help but wonder what he must look like when he was upset.

They had finally reached the white house atop the hill. A few steps away from the porch, Cassie shivered and gasped, feeling as though an electric current had passed from her feet through to her head. Emily gasped as well, it looked as though she had felt it too.

Lysette put a hand on either of the girls' shoulders, "so sorry, dears. I should have mentioned we have quite the strong Masking Barrier surrounding the house. So that the Faeries can't find the house, of course," she added the last part quickly at their blank expressions.

"Of course," Cassie quietly parroted.

Upon entering the roomy foyer, Lysette stifled a yawn. "I'm asleep on my feet," she chuckled, "Vi, dear, could you show the girls to the guest rooms?"

Divina nodded silently and motioned for Cassie and Emily to follow her up the spiraling staircase directly ahead. Cassie stopped at the top of the stairs, tears immediately filling her eyes as she stared at the portrait that hung on the wall there.

It was a large painting, as tall as Cassie and two times as wide, that captured her Grandma Charlotte's likeness perfectly. She was smiling, standing next to a handsome, pudgy older man sitting in a high backed throne. Their robes were both beautiful and ornate, while their crowns, studded with many gemstones, seemed heavy and cold. Warm smiles brightened their kind faces.

Divina stopped too, noticing Cassie's hesitation. "A beautiful portrait, isn't it? It was one of the few things we were allowed to take when we were banished from the castle." She looked into the faces of their grandparents with wonder, "I don't remember them, obviously. As everyone knows, Queen Charlotte left when I was only days old and King Phillip died only a few months after; a broken heart, some say. I hear they were kind and caring rulers."

"I'm a bit rusty on my history, " Cassie began carefully, "did the Faeries take the throne after he passed?"

Divina looked skeptically at them and Cassie worried that perhaps she had crossed a line. She exhaled the breath she had been holding as Divina turned to head down the hall again, calling over her shoulder, "where did you say you two were from? Must be far away if you don't know this story already."

Luckily, Cassie and Emily didn't have to answer the seemingly rhetorical question and Divina continued, "to make a long story short, the day of Daddy's coronation, the Fae Queen was in attendance with a few of her closest members of her court. She stood just as he was about to be crowned and announced that she was the rightful ruler of Lark's Valley before the coronation hall was flooded with Fae soldiers bursting in through the doors and windows."

Divina's eyes were very far away as she recalled what must have been a distressing and traumatic day for her. Suddenly she snapped out of her reverie. "After the ambush, they kept us imprisoned in the dungeon for a few days before the Fae Queen decided to allow us to leave with our lives so long as we went to live amongst our common people as her subjects. Daddy knew we were in no position to bargain so he agreed. This is where we have been ever since; living in the house by the sea; it used to just be our vacation home."

They arrived at the end of the long hallway where two oversized doors rose on opposite walls. Divina turned with a smile on her face, "but, we will never stop fighting for our kingdom. Soon, Daddy will be able to wear his crown again. Now, you two can have these rooms. We can talk more tomorrow!"

They said their good nights and watched as Divina retraced their path, turning the corner and heading out of sight. When she was out of earshot, Cassie turned to her friend.

"Emily..." was all she could manage to say.

"I know." Emily was equally speechless. She muffled a yawn with her hand, "I think we should head to bed." She headed towards the door, "will you be okay tonight?"

Cassie nodded slowly, "goodnight, Em."

The door latched softly leaving Cassie alone in the hallway, but only for a moment. She heard the quiet shuffle of feet coming up the stairs and automatically she turned to see who it was.

Rhett stood at the top of the stairs and leaned against the railing for a moment, looking tired. Slowly, his head lifted and he met her gaze. She smiled, embarrassed for being caught staring. She gently lifted her hand and waved.

He started to make his way over to her and she met him halfway. When they were just a few feet from each other, Cassie spoke up.

"Thank you for sticking up for us earlier and for bringing us here tonight. I think Emily and I would be in a very different situation right now if it wasn't for you."

Rhett stood, lips slightly pursed and brow furrowed. His eyes began to narrow as he took a step closer, whispering, "although you seem harmless and, admittedly, a bit clueless, you and I both know you're hiding something." He took another step forward, "these people here, they are like my family and I won't let anything happen to them. Just remember that. I only brought you to the meeting tonight to keep an eye on you, so don't slip up."

Cassie took an involuntary step back at his intimidating gaze, "I—you don't have to worry. We're here peacefully, truly. I don't want to cause any trouble."

"Good," he smiled, but it was not a light-hearted grin. He started to turn away but stopped to call over his shoulder, "you're welcome, by the way. Sleep well."

~ Five ~

C assie," Emily's soft voice woke Cassie from a particularly deep sleep.

"What time is it?" Cassie groaned, reaching across the bed for her alarm clock that sat on her bedside table. Her hand fell through the air, landing back on the bed, and she sat up feeling confused.

Her eyes began to focus on the room around her and she gasped, taking in the unfamiliar space around her. She forgot she wasn't asleep in her bed, in her room, with her nightstand right where it should be.

Cassie groaned, "so it wasn't a dream then? We're really in some..."

"Magical world!" Emily squealed happily, finishing Cassie's sentence.

Cassie looked at Emily's bright smile and scoffed, "how are you not freaking out about this?"

"This is everything you ever wanted, Cassie." Emily's eyes were sincere, "a family, answers, opportunity! You're my best friend and this is all I've ever wanted for you, too. Of course I'm excited!"

Tears began to wet Cassie's eyes so she smiled brightly, buried her face in her hands and mumbled, "okay, Em, but maybe could we tone the energy down a bit until I wake up more?"

"Got it." Emily chuckled and moved on to the next topic, "so, someone left clothes by our doors last night," she squealed excitedly held out a neatly folded pile of clothing.

"Why is that so exciting?" Cassie chuckled at her friend as she retrieved the clothes and headed toward the attached bathroom.

"Just put them on!" Emily called as the door closed.

Cassie undressed quickly, using the provided supplies to brush her teeth and wash her face; she was happy to find indoor plumbing was a part of this world too. She threw her hair into a loose ponytail and stared at the mound of clothing. She was grateful that someone was kind enough to leave clothes for her and Emily, but these garments were nearly three sizes too big. Cassie knew she wasn't exactly slender, but whoever picked out this outfit clearly didn't pay close enough attention to the sizing.

With a sigh, she threw the too-big clothes over her head and pulled the jeans up, securing them at her waist. So quickly she thought she was imagining it, the fabric on her body began to shrink until the clothing fit her perfectly. In fact, these were the best fitting jeans she'd ever worn.

An unbelieving scoff escaped her lips as she began to examine herself in the mirror, "even the clothes here are magical." She mumbled to herself.

As she walked back into the main room, there was a knock on the bedroom door followed by a sweet voice.

"Girls? Would you like some breakfast?"

Cassie hadn't been here long enough to begin to recognize who the cheerful voice belonged to, so she hurried over to open the door. On the other side was Lysette. She smiled brightly and offered again, pointing down the hallway.

"Breakfast?"

Emily came barreling out the door, "I am *starving*. Where's the food?" her nose sniffed the air the way a hungry dog might do.

Lysette chuckled in unison with Cassie before leading the way down the hall and the spiral staircase towards a large dining room to the left.

The table was stacked high with food—more than necessary for three women, Cassie thought. Breakfast pastries, fresh fruit, meats and more lay steaming on beautifully decorated platters.

As they took their seats, the room began to fill with more people. Cassie recognized Divina, Charles and Rhett, but hadn't seen the others before.

A young, slender woman with beautiful orange hair sat next to Emily. Even from two chairs down Cassie could smell a sweet floral fragrance coming from her. Divina sat gracefully and next to her a tall, handsome boy with glasses took his seat.

Charles and Lysette began filling their plates, and the others followed suit. Cassie had just taken a large bite of cherry danish and Emily was already groaning happily with a full mouth when Charles spoke.

"So, Miss Logan, Miss Williams, I trust our guest accommodations were to your liking?" He smiled kindly.

Cassie swallowed hard, nearly choking, "yeah—" she cleared her throat, starting again attempting to match his formality, "yes, everything was perfect. Thank you, again, for generously bringing us into your home when we had no where else to go."

"You're most welcome to stay as long as you need." Lysette added.

"So," Charles turned to Rhett, "any raids planned for tonight?"

Rhett opened his mouth to reply but was interrupted by Lysette's stern voice, "darling, we agreed, no rebellion-talk at the dinner table."

"In my defense, this is currently the breakfast table." He smiled charmingly then sighed turning back to Rhett, "you can fill me in once we are done here."

"In other news," the handsome boy began speaking, "I finally perfected my potion for water-breathing."

"That's wonderful, Grant," Charles boomed, "how long do the effects last?"

Grant shrunk in his chair a bit, smiling sheepishly, "about five minutes."

"I'm sure you'll break those limits soon, brother." Rhett spoke softly, not looking away from his breakfast, "you're the best Alchemist I know."

"Oh!" The copper-haired girl gasped loudly, making Cassie jump.

"What's wrong, Anthena?" Lysette's voice rose an octave with her concern.

"How rude we are! We haven't formally been introduced to our guests!" She said this the way one might announce the kitchen were on fire. Lysette relaxed, but a slightly annoyed expression remained on her face.

"I'm Anthena, but you can call me Annie. I'm a green witch, so if you have any questions about botany or herbalism, I'm your girl! That's Grant," she pointed her fork across the table, "he's like, a master Alchemist."

"Well..." Grant blushed and shrugged.

"You know King Charles and Queen Lysette, of course, and Princess Divina!" Annie chirped happily.

"Call me Vi, please." Divina smiled politely.

"King Charles is the best swordsman around and Lysette creates the strongest Sigils I've ever seen. And, Rhett is Grant's brother, he's—"

"That's enough, Annie," Rhett said kindly but with finality. Then, softer, "we can't be giving away all of our secrets over breakfast."

Annie didn't skip a beat, turning to Emily, "so, tell me about yourself."

Emily and Annie began a conversation about their common interests—fashion, makeup, and shopping—while other conversations emerged around the table. Rhett and Charles were talking about their most recent training session with some new recruits. Lysette had begun politely asking Grant about his newest concoctions, though her eyes started to glaze over when he passionately dove into details of his newest experiments.

Vi and Cassie were the only two silent. Cassie stole a few glances at her sister who, unlike their mother, seemed engrossed in what Grant had to say. She stared at him intently, almost longingly, for a while, before a slight blush filled her cheeks and a smirk came across her lips. She composed herself quickly, focusing on finishing her breakfast. Vi gulped the last few bites and politely excused herself, nearly running from the room and heading outside.

Annie squealed, "Ooh, Emily, you have to come to my room so I can show you my collection of dresses!"

Emily agreed and stood, waving and shooting a quick, "see ya later, Cassie," behind her as she followed Annie up the stairs. Lysette had stood as well, kissing Charles on the cheek before heading for the door, announcing that she was "heading to the shop for a bit, dear. I'll be back before dinner."

Soon after that, Charles excused himself and somewhere in the middle of everything, Grant had slipped away as well. Once Rhett and Cassie were the only two in the room, he stood, his chair scraping loudly on the floor.

He stared her in the eyes as he spoke, "stick around the house today." He demanded. "It'll be easier to keep an eye on you, besides," he turned to follow after Charles, "it's not safe in the village for a lit-tle girl all alone."

The heat of anger filled Cassie's cheeks as she threw her chair back, taking a few steps toward Rhett. "Hey, I'm not a little girl and you can't just order me around like that!"

Rhett smirked, "can't I? The only way you get freedom is to fight for it." He scoffed and began to exit the room, "as if you could win in a fight against *me*."

"I—Rhett!" She called after him, but he was gone. She groaned in frustration. Who did he think he was? Until just that moment, Cassie hadn't had plans for her day but now a trip to the village sounded lovely.

Cassie stormed out the front door, anger still fueling her steps, when a loud banging claimed her attention. She found herself off course, headed towards the noise at the cliff's edge. There, Vi was wielding a polished sword, brutally attacking a wooden training dummy that was chipped and broken and obviously well-used.

Her movements were so fluid and strong; it was clear she'd been comfortable wielding a sword for quite a while. Her face was calm; just as relaxed as if she were sitting on the couch, reading a good book. Cassie stood, in awe of this warrior-girl in front of her. How could this frightening and lethal person be her sister?

Suddenly Divina stopped, sheathing her sword and catching her breath. She tucked in a few stray hairs that had escaped her long braid. Slowly sat at the cliff's edge, dangling her feet over the end.

Cassie saw an opportunity to talk to Divina alone and struck while the iron was hot. Her original goal of getting to town was gone and replaced with getting to know her sister a bit better. Cassie made her way over to Divina and announced her presence with a cheery voice.

"Hey, Vi!"

Divina smiled quickly but politely before returning her gaze to the vast ocean, "hello."

"You're very good," Cassie began, taking a seat a few steps behind Divina, "with the sword."

"Thank you." she simply replied.

Although Divina didn't seem very conversational, Cassie didn't give up. "So what's your favorite part about living here?"

"Nothing." Divina didn't move her stare from the water, "my family deserves to be back home, in the castle. Ruling fairly and with a kind heart."

"Your family..." Cassie echoed, wondering if one day she might also be able to say *our* family. "You had a sister once, didn't you?"

Divina's head spun so quickly it was as if Cassie had pulled a string attached to Divina's forehead. Her sister's eyes narrowed, and Cassie held her breath; was this another line she wasn't supposed to cross?

"The Lost Princess." Divina's voice remained calm, "I never knew her. We were robbed of the chance."

The wistfulness in Divina's tone gave Cassie the courage to continue, "what if, one day, you got the chance to meet her?"

Divina's response was immediate and her tone was final, "I'd have to kill her, of course."

Cassie's eyes involuntarily widened. "What?"

"Well, for the sake of the world. You know the story," Divina waved her hand in the air dismissively, "when she and I were born, our parents were warned of a prophecy telling that the two of us would bring the end of the world if we remained together. That's why Queen Charlotte volunteered to take one of us away, to save her kingdom." A slight smirk crossed Divina's lips, "that's not just a nighttime story your mom told you, you know. It's the truth."

And just like that, with a few simple sentences Cassie's world was shaken once again. She felt like she had fallen in the ocean, being pummeled with wave after unending wave, gasping for breath and struggling to stay afloat. How many layers were there to this story? How much more could she handle before she hit her limit? Her mouth went dry and her hands clenched in the grass below her. Slowly she realized Vi was staring at her questioningly.

"What's wrong?" Vi asked.

Cassie forced a weak smile and put forth her best nonchalant chuckle, "nothing, everything's fine. I just need to... find a restroom. Breakfast isn't sitting well with me." She stood with wobbly knees, "we'll catch up another time!"

Cassie rushed into the house, taking the stairs two at a time. She turned to the left, hoping she would find Emily quickly. If the people here discovered who Cassie truly was, would Emily then be in danger too?

Cassie banished the thought from her head. After hopelessly passing at least a dozen closed doors, she finally came to a door only half shut, giggles and voices carried out into the hall. She knocked on the door lightly before letting herself in.

"Emily?" She called gently, hoping her panic wasn't clear in her voice.

She rounded the corner finding Emily and Annie fawning over some eccentric and interesting-looking dresses.

"Hey, Cassie!" Emily's face fell when she saw the expression Cassie was wearing, "everything okay?"

"Just a stomach ache,"Cassie told the truth—she was feeling rather nauseated. "Hey, can you help me find something? I just... it's in my room somewhere..."

Emily took the hint. "I'd love to see that shoe collection, Annie, maybe we can meet up again this afternoon?"

Annie was cheerful and polite, "love to! See you later!"

Cassie gripped Emily's hand tightly as they hurried down the hall and into the guest bedroom.

"What's wrong Cassie?" Emily latched the door behind her looking concerned. Cassie paced the middle of the floor.

"Okay, here's what I know," Cassie harshly whispered, "I know this place is definitely real, I know I'm Vi's sister and Lysette and Charles's daughter, and I know my grandma was the Queen who took me away from here for a good reason—to keep me safe."

"Cassie," Emily crossed the room, gently putting her hand on her friend's shoulders, "you're going to have a heart attack if you don't calm down. Sit," she guided Cassie to the end of the bed, "take a breath and give me some more detail here."

Cassie did as she was told and took a deep breath, though it didn't do much good. "They want to kill me!" She blurted.

"Who? Why?" Emily remained calm.

"Things are so much more serious than we thought, Emily. Grandma took me away from Lark's Valley because everyone here believes some prophecy that claims together Vi and I will bring the end of the world. I guess the plan is if they ever found me—the Lost Princess—the only solution would be to kill me to save the world. I—we—have to go home, Emily. They can't know who I really am."

"Wow. Okay." Emily blinked a few times, processing this new information, "well, good news is, they don't know who you are and they don't have to find out. Just stay calm or else we'll seem suspicious for sure. Hey," she smiled cheerily, "Annie was going to take me to a store in town later, maybe you should tag along and take your mind off of this."

"Take my mind off of my life being in danger? That's terrible advice." Cassie shook her head, "I don't think you're understanding the gravity of the situation, Em."

"Look, we can't leave yet. You said it yourself: Charlotte wanted you to find this place; she led you to the door when she came to you in that dream. Just..." Emily's eyes were pleading, "give it one more day here, Cassie, and if you still want to leave tomorrow we will go first thing in the morning. Deal?"

Emily was right. Grandma Charlotte had definitely led her here for a reason. With a shaky sigh, Cassie held her friend's hand tightly, "one more day. But I really don't think I'm going to change my mind, Em."

~ Six ~

Lark's Valley was much different in the day time. The streets were packed with hurrying people, both human and Fae. Humans here looked perfectly normal, just like everyone back home; their fashion seemed to mostly be modern as well .

Cassie was finding that it wasn't challenging to pick out Fae people from the crowd; besides the long ears that tapered off into sharp points at the top, it seemed as though they all had colorful skin, hair, or eyes. Some were particularly beautiful, like a lilac-skinned lady with long white hair braided with small, purple flowers that matched the exact shade of her violet eyes. Others were a bit intimidating, specifically a navy-skinned man with glowing red eyes that sneered at Cassie as she walked past him.

"Keep your eyes down," Annie instructed when she saw Cassie looking around, "it's better to avoid confrontation."

Cassie listened to Annie and kept her eyes down for the most part, however she couldn't help but look up occasionally to take it all in. Even without looking, though, there was a lot to experience. The warm scent of freshly baked bread drifted with the breeze while the sounds of haggling customers and everyday conversations filled the air. Though it was the lack of certain sounds that Cassie noticed the most.

There were no cars or motor vehicles of any kind buzzing around; there weren't any horses riding down the road either. A few people were on bikes, most were walking, but some were flying,—well, floating, really—an unseen force keeping their feet a yard or so above the ground. They held steady at that height, slowly gliding forward.

Cassie looked up just then as a sconce holding a bright green flame caught her eye. It was secured to the door frame of a small store nestled into the wall of a narrow alleyway. The old wooden sign above the door was carved with a name in a language she didn't recognize and the wide double doors below the sign were propped open, beckoning her inside.

Emily and Annie had stopped, causing Cassie to run into Emily's back.

"We're here, come on in," Annie held open the door to what appeared to be a fabric shop.

"You guys go on ahead, I'll catch up in a second." Cassie headed down the back street before the girls could protest. She was alone in the alley, away from the hustle and bustle of the busy street.

She cautiously entered the store which was equally as empty as the alleyway; not even a soul sat behind the counter. The shop was lit solely by candlelight; several candles with a thick amount of melted-wax buildup were carefully placed in strategic spots to ensure the best lighting possible. Still, it took Cassie's eyes a moment to fully adjust.

"Hello?" She called, receiving no response. Perhaps the clerk had just stepped in the back for a moment.

There were a great many shelves and tables packed into the small space, each filled with an assortment of items. Even in the dimness of the candlelight the trinkets, jewelry and raw-cut gemstones glistened. Dried herbs hung in bunches for sale along one wall and questionable liquids filled an assortment of jars along the other wall.

As she made her way deeper into the store, she found a small round table with four identical rings on it. Each ring was made of a polished white metal, twisted into ornate designs. In the center of each ring was a different gemstone, each as beautiful as the one before it.

Cassie was certainly no gemstone expert, but she recognized the topaz, ruby, sapphire and emerald stones when she saw them. Her eye was drawn to her favorite stone—the bright, cheerful topaz. Her grandma had gotten her a topaz necklace when she was young that she had refused to take off for the longest time. She picked up the ring to get a closer look.

The perfectly polished stone drew her in; its facets glittered charmingly. The yellow stone entangled in the white metal reminded Cassie of a bright midday sun peaking out from behind fluffy clouds. She no more than turned the ring over in her hand when a clattering behind her grabbed her attention. Cassie spun around just in time to see the towering, green creature as it closed its oversized hand around her wrist. She gasped in shock, trying to free her hand with no success.

The creature's skin reminded her of an alligator, but with a thin layer of blond hair covering it. He was tall, and wide, with arms the size of small tree trunks. Two, long, blackened tusks protruded from a severe underbite. Its beady yellow eyes bore into hers as he roared, his foul-smelling breath blowing her hair back.

"What do we have here?" His voice was low and slow, "a thief! You dare steal from me?"

"No, no! Sir, I'm not a thief—really, I—" Cassie groaned in pain when his vice-like grip tightened, lifting her from the ground so that they were face to face.

He plucked the ring from her hand, "no use for thieves," he grumbled, "and you're not fat enough to make a good meal..."

Cassie struggled in vain, pounding his arm with her free fist with all of her strength—he didn't even seem to notice.

"Let me go, please," she begged, "I wasn't stealing, I swear!"

"Better yet," he said, ignoring her pleas, "I'll just make sure you can't steal anything ever again." He pulled a long knife from the belt at his waist; the dirty blade was crooked and sharp.

Before he could make another move, a blur of red flashed across Cassie's vision, replaced by the glint of metal as a knife appeared by the creature's throat.

Moving lightning-fast, Rhett had himself clinging to the monster's back, a blade in his hand digging into the skin of the creature's neck.

"Drop the knife, troll, or your next breath will be your last." His voice was strong and impossible to ignore.

Cassie's heart was still racing a mile a minute, but she found a slight bit of relief in seeing Rhett. When the troll finally sighed and loosened his grip, Cassie yanked her hand back, rubbing her sore wrist.

"Cassie, go." Rhett ordered, still holding the knife to the troll's jugular.

Cassie didn't hesitate and ran out into the alley. She stood there, unsure where to go next, when Rhett calmly sauntered out a moment later.

"It's interesting," he began, sheathing his knife, "I could have sworn I told you not to come out today."

While Cassie was truly grateful to Rhett for saving his life, she could not stand being talked down to. The chill of fear was quickly replaced by the heat of anger while Rhett stood waiting for a response.

"You're not wrong. But I don't have to listen to you." *Great*, she thought, *now I sound like a pouty five year old.*

"Clearly you should have listened to me," his calm demeanor was fading, "you were *this close* to being killed in there."

"Oh please," she scoffed taking a step closer, "I had everything completely under control." They both knew she was lying, but she kept a stubborn face, daring him to call her out.

He took the bait, "oh, my bad. Please, tell me, what were you going to do when you lost that hand?"

Cassie was spared from answering when Emily and Annie appeared from the street.

"Hey guys!" Annie called, oblivious to the ensuing argument, "Rhett, nice of you to join us. We're going to grab some lunch, wanna come with?"

"You two go on," Rhett's calm facade was back, "Cassie and I have some errands of our own to run."

Emily leaned around Annie's shoulder, meeting Cassie's gaze with a look that asked, *is everything okay?*

Although she had no idea what "errands" Rhett was referring to, she knew she wasn't done with their conversation, at the very least. Cassie nodded, answering Emily's silent question.

For good measure she plastered a smile on her face and added, "yeah we'll meet you back at the house later."

As soon as Emily and Annie were out of sight, Rhett began walking the opposite direction. "Come on. There's something you need to see."

Cassie followed, her curiosity getting the best of her. They wound their way through a few more empty alleys before merging back into the busy street traffic. Cassie was just about to ask where they were headed when she was interrupted by a commotion down on the corner.

As a young human couple walked into a store, two Fae men rushed them from behind, dragging the couple to the ground by the back of their shirts.

"Rhett—" Cassie looked over at him to see he was already watching as one of the Fae men ripped the woman's satchel from her arms, dumping out the contents before crushing it all with a stomp of his heavy boots.

The human man attempted to come to his girlfriend's aid, but he was thrown to the ground again. This time the Fae descended as well, fists pummeling and feet kicking the poor man who had curled himself into a ball, trying to protect his face.

"Rhett!" Cassie said with more urgency, "do something!"

She looked around astonished that the passersby turned their heads the other way, simply rerouting their paths around the ruckus.

When Rhett continued to stand, stoic, Cassie scoffed and took a step towards the scuffle. Rhett grabbed her wrist, holding her in place.

"It's not our fight," he said.

Horrified, Cassie saw the man begin to go limp, his girlfriend pounding in vain on the assailants' backs. Just then a pair of Fae soldiers rounded the corner. With a sigh of relief, Cassie watched the soldiers walk right up to the fight—surely they would put an end to this.

Instead, the Fae men stopped beating the nearly unconscious man, and received little more than a nod from the soldiers as they continued on their course.

In disbelief, Cassie watched the scene come to a close, the human girl crying as she tended to her boyfriend while the guards wore a smirk on their faces, sparing not even a glance in the poor couple's direction.

"Cassie," Rhett's voice was quiet but strong, his green eyes burning with intensity, "that was nothing. Nothing compared to the injustices that happen every day under the Fae Queen's rule. That fight might not have been ours, but people like those two are exactly who we fight for. One day, the Larken family will rule again to put an end to horrible crimes like that once and for all." His voice softened, "that was why I didn't want you to come to town alone today—it's not safe for a defenseless human girl in Lark's Valley anymore."

Shocked and nauseated, Cassie only nodded her head to show she understood. She was thankful when Rhett didn't release her wrist—she wasn't sure she could have walked on her own accord—but led her out of town and back to the Larken's seaside home on the cliff.

* * *

After a hot mug of chamomile tea, Cassie was finally ready to tell Emily about what had happened in town earlier that day. The girls were in Emily's bed, comfy in their borrowed pajamas. Cassie quickly summarized the events, shuddering as she remembered the troll's foul breath and the looks on the helpless couple's faces.

"It's a good thing Rhett was there then, huh? Doesn't hurt that he's easy on the eyes." Emily waggled her eyebrows.

Cassie scoffed, hiding her smirk, "Em, can't you take anything seriously?"

Emily pretended to think about that question, "nope. Probably not!" She smiled, then gently put her hand on Cassie's shoulder. "You sure you're okay? I could sleep in your room tonight if you want."

"I'm fine. Really, thank you for listening," Cassie lifted the empty mug in her hand, "I'd better get this back to the kitchen. Goodnight, Em."

Cassie quietly slipped out into the hall; everyone was already in bed and it would be quite rude to wake them. She tiptoed down the stairs and slowly placed the dirty mug in the sink before slinking back through the kitchen door. The orange flickering of a burning fire caught her eye, beckoning her into the adjacent living room.

There she found Rhett lounging on a couch staring into the roaring fire. He didn't acknowledge her entrance, but Cassie knew that he was aware that she was there.

He had disappeared after getting Cassie safely home, leaving a lot unsaid between them.

Cassie couldn't help but blurt the question that had been burning in her mind all afternoon, "what were you doing in that store today?"

"Watching you." He said without emotion.

"Why?" She pressed.

"I told you. It wasn't safe in town."

"No," she said, not accepting that answer. She rephrased the question, "your motivation. What was it?"

There was a moment of silence before his response, "I feel responsible for you. You wouldn't be here if I hadn't brought you to the meeting that night so now I have to watch you."

"Well I release you from your responsibilities," she stood, arms crossed in the doorway. "Just leave me alone from here on out." She turned to leave.

"Why are you here?"

She stopped in her tracks. Did she have a good answer for that question? It was one she'd been asking herself for a while now. Slowly, and choosing her words carefully, she replied.

"I feel like I have responsibilities, too. I think I have to help the Larkens. My grandma would have wanted me to."

With that, Rhett let her leave. She trudged back up the stairs to her bedroom. The question he had asked her kept repeating in her mind, like a broken record.

What she had told him was the truth—she did feel like Grandma Charlotte brought her here to help her family. However, she felt deep down that there was more to this story. She worried, though, that while digging up the past she might also unearth something better left buried.

~ Seven ~

When Annie invited Emily and Cassie out on a foraging trip to the forest nearby, Cassie eagerly agreed. She had decided the previous night that she wasn't going to let fear drive her back home, but she really didn't want to stay cooped up in the same house as Rhett all day.

Cassie ripped the leaves off of a plant Annie had said needed harvesting, and she threw them in her woven basket. There was just something about Rhett that irked her to no end.

How could one person be so calm all of the time, but then flip a switch and become enraged and intense in an instant? His mood swings gave her whiplash. Where did he get off ordering her around and stalking her and then making it seem as though he were only concerned with her safety? He was nothing to her, and she nothing to him. What was it going to take to get him to leave her alone?

"Um, Cassie?" Annie's voice was kind, but concerned, "let's try to be a bit more gentle with the plants, okay? Their potency in spells and potions really begins in the way they're grown but can be affected in many ways, including the intention with which you harvest them."

Cassie started to use a more gentle approach to plucking the leaves from the stem and Annie smiled in approval.

"That's better! We'll be giving this to Grant later so he can use it to make a calming, anti-anxiety potion so we should keep that intention in mind while taking the leaves with us."

Emily had efficiently cleared her portion of the plant of leaves, "what else will we be gathering today, Annie?"

A crunch of twigs behind them made the girls jump.

"Oh," Annie said, relieved to see that it was only Grant, Vi, and Rhett making their way towards them, "you scared me!" she scolded them.

Grant blushed, "apologies, Annie, I only wanted to bring some more help since you were doing this favor for me."

Cassie's scowl deepened when she saw Rhett. There was just no escaping him. She walked further into the forest, following the long, winding plant and gently gathering more of its leaves as she went. Soon, she was far enough away that their chatter became nothing more than background noise.

She took a deep breath, focusing on calming herself down. Cassie let her mind wander, smiling as she remembered the days she spent with her grandmother in the forest around their home. They would spend hours gathering wild strawberries and flowers for tea.

Grandma Charlotte had been sure to teach Cassie which plants to stay away from and which ones to carefully gather. They'd get home and happily munch on their berry harvest while stringing up the herbs and flowers to dry in the kitchen.

"If we treat the earth well," Grandma Charlotte had always said, "it will reward us with a beautiful and useful bounty. Be kind and respect nature, always, my little lark."

Cassie brought herself back to reality, quickly realizing she had wandered a bit too far and could no longer see the group she left behind.

"Emily?" she called.

She heard a faint reply in the distance, "Cassie?"

A rustling in the tree above froze her in her tracks. Slowly she turned, letting out a squeal of fear when she came face to face with a massive spider-like creature that had descended from the branches above.

The arachnid stood a full two feet taller than her and its body was as least three times her size. With a snake-like hiss, the spider took a step forward, each of its eight legs moving in sync and its mouth opening in anticipation of its next meal.

Cassie managed to let out a scream, which only incited a louder hiss from the creature as it tensed its body in preparation to spring. Cassie reached around blindly for anything she might use to protect herself. She grasped a fallen tree branch so huge that she had to use both hands to wield it, and held it up like a baseball bat.

The spider sprung—it was unfathomably fast. It was only sheer luck that Cassie was able to swing and hit the spider on the side of the head, sending it staggering to the left while her rotten weapon exploded into a million wooden fragments.

The creature recovered much faster than she did and was on the move again, ready for a second attack. Cassie saw that she had no other option than to run. She scurried backwards, tripping on the root of an old tree. The spider was over top of her now, rearing up on its hind legs to put as much force into the dive as possible.

Cassie closed her eyes tight, unable to watch what she knew was going to happen next.

A loud thud and the vibration of something heavy hitting the ground made Cassie open her eyes. Almost as soon as she did, she was being lifted to her feet none too gently by a strong pair of hands.

"What were you thinking wandering so far?" Rhett scolded helping brush the dirt from her shoulders, "are you alright?"

She nodded her head, watching as Vi wiped her sword clean of the dead spider's blood. Grant stood over the spider, pushing his glasses up on his nose, and examining the monstrous corpse. Annie and Emily weren't far behind, though they moved much slower than these trained warriors.

"What a wonderful discovery!" Grant exclaimed as Annie and Emily rushed to Cassie's side, pushing past Rhett who quietly stepped out of the way. "This Giant Spider venom will be perfect for a poison."

He had removed a small vile from his pocket and was busy extracting a yellowish liquid from the spider's fangs. "Only takes a drop or two from a mature specimen such as this one to kill a fully grown man. You're extremely lucky to be alive, Cassie. How did you manage to escape its grasp?"

Cassie swallowed, though her mouth was dry. "I hit it with a branch."

"A branch?" Rhett scoffed, arms crossed.

"Sounds like you need your own weapon." Vi smiled kindly.

"I—" Cassie stuttered, "Well, I wouldn't even know where to begin, I've never been much for... swords."

"You're certainly going to need to learn if you're going to be a part of this rebellion. We have no use for unskilled members. Same goes for you, Emily." Vi's words were strong, but not unkind. "What talents do you two have?"

When the girls stood, silent, Vi only smiled again, "don't worry. I'd be happy to train you with a sword."

Grant, finished with his venom-extraction, turned to Cassie, "it wouldn't hurt to learn a bit about Alchemy either. You should study with me as well."

"Oh!" Annie jumped giddily, "I could show you everything I know about casting spells. This will be such fun!"

"You guys have already given us a place to stay, food to eat, even these clothes on our backs. To ask you for more..." Cassie held her arms close to her body to stop them from shaking.

"Nonsense," Grant spoke as he moved closer to Vi, "as Annie said, it will be enjoyable to share our talents with eager students."

"Being a part of our rebellion means we ask a lot from you," Vi explained, smiling up at Grant, "my family and I try to give back in any way we can, and it still may never be enough to repay you for asking you to put your lives in danger."

"Besides," Rhett finally spoke up turning to Cassie, "you seem to be a magnet for trouble with no self defense skills. I wouldn't turn down an offer for help if I were you."

Cassie was speechless, but Emily could only squeal with glee, "this is so wonderful, thank you! Cassie and I will be the best students."

As she looked around the group, Cassie noticed the basket she had been using to gather plants had been crushed in the struggle.

"Don't worry about that," Annie spoke softly following her line of sight, "between all of us, we've collected more than enough for Grant's project."

"In fact," Grant's eyes lit up, "Cassie, Emily, you two should join me as I prepare my potions. We'll consider it your first lesson."

* * *

Cassie was exhausted after the adrenaline rush from her experience in the forest, but luckily making potions didn't seem to require too much physical movement. She and Emily sat in chairs opposite Annie and Grant, who stood hunched over a long metal work bench cluttered with ingredients and supplies.

Grant's space in the basement of the Larken's home was lit by candle-like sticks giving off a luminous white light. However, Cassie was shocked to see there was no flame burning on a wick or electricity running through a filament. She wondered where the light was coming from, but didn't want to speak up and ask to find out.

Shelves, tables and cupboards filled the room, each serving the purpose of holding Grant's bottles, jars, dried plants and other useful items. The smell of floral incense swirled in the air adding to the ambiance.

Currently, Grant was preparing the fresh plant material they had gathered earlier by removing any leftover stems from the leaves and cleaning them with water in a bowl before handing the dripping leaves over to Annie.

"Now that the materials are clean they are ready to be dehydrated. Annie will take care of that with a simple spell, then we can grind them into a fine powder with these," he cheerily held up a mortar and pestle.

Cassie and Emily watched in awe as Annie laid the wet leaves across the table, holding her hands out over them, palms down. She closed her eyes and breathed deeply, maintaining a constant rhythm of inhales and exhales.

Cassie could see her lips moving quickly as she muttered the spell to herself. There were no sparks or flashes of light, nor odors or gusts of wind as Annie cast her spell. Yet the leaves slowly shriveled and became brittle, dried herbs for Grant's potion. He quickly scooped them up into the mortar setting it and the pestle in front of Cassie.

"Here," he explained, "grind these until there are no big chunks left; the powder must easily dissolve into the liquid. Now, where did I put that jar?"

Grant scurried around the crowded room throwing open cupboard doors and searching through overly full shelves while Cassie did her best to crush the leaves with the pestle. It didn't take long for the extremely dry plant material to disintegrate into a fine powder and by the time Cassie was done, Grant had found what he was searching for.

Grant held a large blue-tinted jar with an equally large cork in the top holding in at least a gallon of crystal clear water.

"So, why do you need the water from that particular jar when there's a tap with fresh water upstairs?" Emily asked.

Grant chuckled, pushing his glasses further up his nose, "you see, potions get their power from the rituals you do as you make them, the symbolism behind the ingredients you choose, and the power of your own mind. This water is special because I spent three days hiking in the mountains to find it with the intention of using it for this exact purpose."

He held the jar at arms length, looking at it as if it were the most precious thing he had ever seen, "this water comes from the melted snow in the calmest place in this world: the peaks of Mount Sahreen. Up there, you'll find a plateau filled with the most crystalline, undisturbed snow. It's never windy, stormy, or in any way agitated. Water from such a tranquil place is the perfect addition to a calming potion such as the one we're making today."

He grabbed a decorative double edged knife from its stand on a shelf, "we'll be using this athame to mix our potion because it was gifted to me by someone who loves me, and that makes it an exceedingly valuable tool."

Without skipping a beat, he dashed to find more powders and liquids, throwing them all into the jar of his highly prized water. He took the powder Cassie had just ground, dumping it into the jar as well, "and the finishing touch! Now, when we stir a potion it's crucial to remember these rules: Stir clockwise when you're making a potion with projective energy such as manifesting, increasing, or wishing. Stir in a counterclockwise direction if you are making a potion with receptive energy like releasing or banishing. Today we will stir which direction to make a potion that will bring peace to the user?"

"Clockwise." Cassie said confidently.

"Yes," Grant said cheerily, using his athame to stir the mixture in a clockwise direction. "Perhaps the most important part of Alchemy isn't the ingredients or tools you use, but your intention and purpose. During every step of the process you must keep in mind the reason you're creating this potion. Think peaceful, calming thoughts while harvesting, preparing, mixing and finally," he dumped the contents into a pot hanging over an open fire in the hearth behind where Cassie sat, "heating your potion."

Steam began to rise from the pot as the contents boiled becoming light green in color, "I'm making this potion for someone special to me. The love I have for her will make the magic even more potent."

It was fascinating to Cassie the way all four elements played a part in the creation of this one potion. The earth was represented in the plants and water with the melted snow. The flames in the hearth and the smoke that swirled all around brought the elements fire and air into the equation.

"My favorite part about potions is their variety of uses," Annie chimed in, "in this case the potion will be taken internally by the user, as most potions are, but potions can also be used for anointing people and things, scrying—"

"which is also known as seeing the future," Grant interrupted.

"—and even in beauty rituals! I use one of Grant's potions in my bathwater every night to help keep my skin hydrated and healthy."

It was clear to Cassie that Grant was an immensely accomplished Alchemist. "It must have taken you years to get so skilled in this art, Grant." Cassie mused.

"It was the family business. My father was a master at this craft and I picked it up quickly from watching him every day." Grant pulled a decorative crystal bottle from under the table. The stopper at the top was a polished purple amethyst, and the crystal itself was a pale purple as well. He slowly funneled his completed potion into the bottle, sealing it with smile on his face.

"And that's that," he said, "Alchemy may have a lot of steps and details in its process, but it is a very useful skill that anyone can easily learn with a little practice and dedication."

"Thank you for the lesson, Grant. It was really fun watching you work." Emily said.

"I feel like I should have been taking notes." Cassie admitted, "you make it look so easy."

"Well, here," Grant ran over to a bookshelf in the corner, selecting a thick tomb and handing it to Cassie. The title read, *Alchemy: the complete guide to potions, elixirs and poisons,* "this will help with your studies."

"With that, I think it's time for dinner!" Annie stood from her seat and headed for the stairs. Emily and Cassie followed close behind.

When Grant didn't move from his spot, Cassie turned around letting the others go on ahead.

"You coming, Grant?"

A solemn look fell over his face as he took the small yellow vile of spider venom out from his coat's inner pocket, "I think I'll be missing dinner tonight, ladies. I've got a poison to make."

"Is something wrong?" Cassie asked carefully, feeling a bit bewildered from seeing his mood change so quickly. She thought of Rhett, and his mood swings.

Grant looked over with sad eyes, "it upsets me to see magic used for harmful purposes, but, unfortunately, when you're in the middle of a war it can be a necessary evil while fighting for what is right. The poison I'm making will cover many of our warrior's weapons, and many lives will be taken," he shook his head sadly, "with this tiny vile, I'll kill hundreds."

* * *

Cassie was startled awake the next morning by her door being thrown open, slamming against the wall. The shock sent her over the edge of the bed while she remained wrapped helplessly in the blankets.

She scrambled to get loose, just getting her head free as a heavy metal sword fell onto the floor next to her. Cassie took a moment, still wrapped up like a burrito, to look over at the sword. She then glanced upward to find Vi staring down at her, arms crossed over her torso.

"Get up," she said sternly, "your first sword training lesson starts in ten minutes." Vi began to head to Emily's room, "you won't like the consequences of being late, so get dressed. I'll see you outside."

Cassie groaned and fidgeted her way out of the blanket prison. She rose, slowly, and reached for the sword, shocked when she felt the weight of the weapon in her hand.

With a grunt, she lifted the sword and held it out in front of her wondering if she would even be able to practice with something so heavy in the first place, let alone harm another living thing with it.

She banished the thought from her mind and scurried to the wardrobe—which had been fully furnished by Annie, each item enchanted to fit the wearer perfectly—and chose the most plain, comfortable and tight fitting clothes she could find. Cassie didn't know much about sword fighting but she could easily assume one didn't want loose clothing for their opponent to be able to grab onto.

Cassie nearly flew down the stairs, doing her best to keep the sword from dragging on the ground, and threw herself out the front door. She found Vi and Emily waiting for her.

Vi stifled a chuckle, glancing back and forth between Cassie and Emily, "it seems we need to do some strength training before jumping right into sword practice. Try holding that above your head."

Cassie did as she was instructed, managing to lift the sword with shaky arms. She smiled sheepishly, lowering the sword, "I don't normally do much heavy lifting."

This time Vi didn't hold back the laughter, "you think that's heavy? I've got my work cut out for me with these two, that's for sure."

Vi had moved her attention to something behind the girls. Cassie turned to look just as Rhett came into view. He wore the smile of a man with a trick up his sleeve. Her eyes narrowed; what was he up to?

"I could have told you that." He held out his hand, asking for the sword. Cassie handed it to him, "it's going to take a lot of work on your part Cassie, but it will be worth it. Let's show her what she's working towards, eh, Vi?"

Rhett drew the sword up and swung it at Vi. She jumped backwards, a huge smile on her face. Without another word, she held her sword up as well, advancing towards Rhett with an expression and stance reminiscent of a lioness on the hunt.

Their fight looked more like a dance. Both of them were clearly skilled with their swords, and Cassie marveled at how strong they must be, whipping their weapons through the air as if they were as light as a twig.

Rhett lunged and Vi dodged. He swung the sword over his head and she blocked the blow effortlessly. Her defense was perfect and his offense was merciless. In just a split second, however, their roles reversed, Vi began throwing the blows while Rhett defended himself against them.

Cassie watched in awe as the two of them continued to go strong, neither seeming to be getting tired but neither making any progress, either. A small gasp escaped Cassie's lips as Rhett jumped to the side, positioning himself behind Vi. She spun, sword ready for a counter-attack but was just a second too slow. Rhett had already placed his weapon perfectly, the tip of it pointing directly where Vi's heart sat in her chest.

The look of glee fell from Vi's face, replaced with shock while Rhett's grin deepened. He straightened up, letting his sword fall to his side.

"Enough play." Vi didn't hide her disappointment from losing. She turned to Cassie and Emily, ignoring Rhett altogether, "time to train, let's do a few laps down on the beach. We'll work to build up your endurance first, then we can get those arms of yours strong enough to hold a sword."

Vi slid her weapon into a sheath attached to a belt at her waist, then reached to the ground below her where two more identical belts sat. She tossed one to Cassie, the other to Emily, "put this on. It will be good to get used to the feeling of having a sword at your side while running." Without another word, she headed down the hill.

Rhett sauntered to Cassie, sliding her sword into its home at her hip. Startled at his closeness, she simply stared at him as he whispered, "good luck. Now that I've got her upset, you three should have a *splendid* time together."

She groaned internally, looking out to the endless ocean beyond the cliff. Cassie inhaled deeply as the sun peeked over the pink clouds on the horizon, casting a few orange rays of light across the dark water. With a sigh, she began jogging down the hill to catch up with Vi and Emily. Somehow she knew today was going to be a long one.

~ Eight ~

Cassie and Emily soon found themselves developing a routine while staying at the Larken's home. During their first few weeks, their days mostly consisted of sword lessons from Vi and getting to know the rest of their house mates, while their nights were filled with Alchemy lessons with Grant.

It was easy to forget the world they left behind, with noisy mechanics, horrible pollutants, and an utter lack of excitement. Unlike the electric and fuel-powered world they grew up in, life in Lark's Valley was powered by all-natural magic.

There were no need for light bulbs when you could summon a glowing ball of energy with a snap of your fingers. The people here had no desire to invent cars or even domesticate horses for travel. Magic got them where they needed to go with flying, teleportation, and potions that would prevent you from getting tired so you could walk for miles with no end.

Phones had never been invented either since people here communicated through sending letters that would appear directly in front of its recipient, relaying any written text, photo, or voice message the sender enchanted it with.

Cassie couldn't imagine going back to her non magical world—not ever. Emily had no reason to return either, and seemed to be adapting to the magical environment extremely well.

For Cassie, it wasn't so much of an adaptation to the world, but a feeling of finally finding home. Everything simply felt right here in Lark's Valley—not to mention she hadn't felt this in touch with her grandmother since she had passed, and her heart soared with happiness.

Cassie was eager to learn all she could as quickly as she could and was pleasantly surprised to find how easily she was picking it all up. She had to remind herself often: magic was in her blood, after all.

After another long night of Alchemy lessons with Grant in his "laboratory", as he affectionately called it, the girls sat in bed drinking Cassie's favorite nighttime beverage; chamomile tea with flowers picked fresh from Annie's garden.

"I feel like I've been hit by a truck," Cassie groaned, "Vi's workouts are intense."

"I bet! She seems like a tough teacher but you have to admit: it's so rewarding now that we're able to finally lift a sword without straining so much," Emily finished the last of her tea, "Cassie," her voice dropped to a whisper, "I'm really glad you didn't decide to go home. I can see us having a real future here."

Before Cassie could reply, there was a knock on the door.

"Ladies!" Annie called, "I'm coming in!"

"What's up Annie?" Emily stood from the bed.

"Lysette and Charles are out of town for some business. We're all having a bonfire down at the beach. You two deserve a break after studying so diligently these past couple weeks. Come with me!"

If Cassie had been honest, she much rather would have stayed in bed under the covers with her Alchemy book and mug of tea. Instead, she didn't want to deflate the excitement that was quickly blooming on Emily's face and agreed to go.

Less than ten minutes later, Cassie was walking barefoot in the cold sand wearing a comfy hoodie and jeans. The bonfire sat in the middle of the beach and was unlike any other she had seen before.

Odd shapes and bold colors danced within the flames, which she soon saw were being controlled by a couple of pyromancers. They told stories with their fire, depicting people running and sword fighting, then dancing and celebrating; clearly they had won whatever fiery battle they were in.

There were many people here that she didn't recognize, though they were all around her age. Emily and Annie had run off to chat with Grant and Vi who were standing near the water's edge. Grant's hands were around Vi's waist, hers wrapped around his neck, while they laughed and smiled at each other.

Cassie stood alone, feeling awkward and wishing she had just stayed in bed like she had wanted to. Then, among the moving bodies surrounding the bonfire, she saw one that was sitting perfectly still.

Rhett sat on a long piece of driftwood, forearms resting on his knees, hands clasped in front of him as he stared into the fire. She hadn't seen him around much the past couple days. Cassie had assumed he had finally decided to leave her alone as he began to see he had no reason to worry about her.

Being as he was the only one nearby that she knew, Cassie decided to see if he wanted some company. Their track record hadn't been the best but she was feeling great after this past successful week and had proven to herself that change wasn't impossible. Perhaps this was an opportunity to change the awful start they had gotten off to.

"Hey, Rhett." Cassie approached slowly, "can I sit with you?"

He glanced up at her and nodded once, "go for it."

She sat down, feeling the warmth of the flames on her face. *So far so good*, she said to herself, *now just... say something. Anything. Just mention... something like—*

"My brother mentioned you're doing well with his Alchemy lessons. " Rhett glanced sideways at her.

Cassie breathed a sigh of relief—she hated having to start conversations. "Yeah, um, he's a wonderful teacher and I've been really enjoying the lessons," she took a deep breath, "so there's something I've actually been really curious about."

"Yeah?" He raised his eyebrows.

She blurted her thoughts while she still had the courage, "your hair. It's just so... *red* and *long*."

Rhett chuckled, clearly not offended by the question. "Not very inconspicuous is it? Just the way I was born. The red is all natural and the length, well, Faeries don't cut their hair unless they're mourning. Thankfully I haven't had anything to mourn lately. But yeah, being half Faerie makes me look a bit different," he ran his fingers across the tip of his ear.

"So all Faeries have colored hair and pointed ears?"

"Not all Fae have different colored hair but they all have something inhuman about them besides just the pointed ears; different colored skin, hair, eyes. I know a woman whose veins in her skin look like the veins in a leaf and another who's tongue is forked like a snake. I think I was lucky to only get red hair and slightly pointed ears—it made growing up with a fully human brother easier."

She couldn't help but smile; this was the most he'd talked to her and he seemed pleasant. She felt the conversation coming more organically now as she asked, "so tell me more about your family. Grant is your half brother, right? Where are your parents?"

He shifted his weight, leaning more towards her, "my mother, Dahlia, was a Faerie and Grant's mother was a human, like our father, Edward. Our parents are passed away now. My mother died in childbirth and that's when my father re-married, and Grant was born."

He began to smile as he reminisced, "my father made potions—the best potions in the kingdom. Until one day a slight slip of the hand caused his shop to explode, killing him and Grant's mother. Later we discovered it wasn't just a careless mistake that caused the explosion, but a Faerie sabotage. That was only a few years ago. Soon after that I found out about the rebellion and joined the cause. This is where I've been ever since. What about your family?"

She told him the truth, "the only family I've ever known is my grandmother but she recently passed away too, last year. Emily is kinda like my family too, now. I don't know what I'd do without her."

"You said your grandmother would want you to help the Larkens. Why?"

Cassie paused for a moment, taking the time to chose her words carefully. She didn't want to lie but she didn't want to reveal anything that might make Rhett suspicious about who she really was, either.

"That's just the kind of person she was. Always caring and kind and she knew a good cause when she saw one. I think she passed that on to me. I can see you're all good people fighting for the right thing and I want to be a part of that."

A happy squeal drew their attention away. Grant was chasing Vi across the beach, both were wearing huge grins. He scooped her up by the waist, taking them both down to the ground where they rolled in the sand, and the joyful cries continued.

"So, your brother and Vi, huh?"

Rhett sighed, "the Princess isn't supposed to be with him, so they usually keep it under wraps, but on nights like tonight when her parents aren't around they're allowed to be a bit less cautious. As his brother, of course I want him to be happy," Rhett rubbed the back of his neck, looking sadly in their direction, "but I can't help feeling this will end badly for him. When the Larkens are back on the throne, I worry he's going to get left behind."

One of the novice pyromancers that had been messing with the bonfire was starting to become a bit careless. With one wrong wave of his hand, the flames soared twenty feet in the air, then waved wildly around like a garden hose with too much pressure and no one holding it steady.

Everyone in the vicinity threw themselves to the ground or ran in the other direction, but Cassie's reflexes weren't quite so developed. She stared in shock and horror as the snake-like flame whipped toward her. In the blink of an eye, she was no longer sitting on the driftwood with Rhett. Instead, he had dove behind the piece of wood taking her with him.

After finding her breath again, she blinked a few times trying to get her bearings. A moment later she realized she was lying right on top of Rhett. He patiently and kindly waited for her to catch up to the situation before trying to move her.

"You alright?" He asked with concern in his voice as he pushed her hair out of her face, trying to better examine her. She sat, frozen, mesmerized by the closeness of him just as she had been the other day. Only this time, he was close enough that she could smell the scent of him; pine mixed with something spicy and a bit of campfire smoke that lingered on his shirt...

Cassie cleared her throat, "yeah, I'm fine. Um, thank you."

"Of course," he made no move to get up and Cassie wasn't going to either until she heard Emily's shrill voice call out among the crowd.

"Cassie!"

Cassie scrambled to her feet, waving her hand in the air, "I'm fine, Em!" She looked over at Rhett who was brushing sand from his clothes, "I'd better get over there. It was, um, really nice talking with you tonight." She smiled brightly, her grin widening when he returned the sentiment with a dazzling smile of his own.

The pyromancer was apologizing profusely to anyone who would listen, swearing that he had no clue how that could have happened and insisting he'd been studying that spell for months.

Cassie ignored his apologies and went to stand next to Emily, who wore a teasing look on her face, "what was that about?" Emily nodded towards Rhett who had begun walking towards the house.

"What was what?"

"That smile. That was a flirty smile and don't you try to deny it!"

Cassie's attempt at an effortless scoff came out more as a nervous snort, "flirty? With Rhett? You're crazy if you think I'd ever be interested in him... I mean, just...look at him!"

"Yeah, I know, super hot, right?"

Cassie jokingly punched her friend in the arm, trying to laugh it off, though, she had to admit, Emily wasn't wrong. Even though part of her agreed with her friend, there was no reason Emily had to know that.

* * *

The near-black waves of the ocean soared and crashed in the storm's gale. Cassie pictured the gulls that normally played in the updrafts struggling to navigate the strong winds while the fish and Merpeople living below the surface had no clue what was raging above them. Of course, she had no proof that Merpeople even existed but it really didn't seem so far-fetched, considering everything else she'd encountered here so far.

Rain poured outside, each droplet sounding like fingernails tapping on the glass of the window Cassie had perched herself in front of. She decided to stare out of this particular window at the end of the hallway, between her room and Emily's, because it had the best view of the ocean.

She sighed, watching the torrent continue to wreak its havoc on the outside world as she pulled closed the fluffy cardigan she wore, reveling in its warmth. Today was the perfect day to curl up under the blankets with a mug of her favorite chamomile tea and a good book while a fire burned in the hearth. With that thought, Cassie realized today was the first day in nearly a month without any kind of training or lessons on her schedule.

Grant was off in search of the perfect place to collect rain water for his potions, and Vi was with him simply because she wanted to be. Her excuse to her parents was simply that she had nothing better to do, since the weather outside was not ideal for sword practice.

Annie and Emily were off having a magical spa day—apparently they had been working on potions for their hair, skin, and nails and decided today was a good day to use them—so here Cassie stood, alone, staring at the deadly water slamming angrily against the shore.

"What are you doing?"

Cassie spun around. Rhett stood a few feet away, dressed in fitted dark jeans and a black v-neck shirt. He tucked a stray strand of his bright red hair behind his ear, and smiled as she met his gaze. She replied with a smile of her own.

"Nothing," she answered honestly, "just staring out at the downpour," Rhett came to stand next to her, their bodies side by side filling the width of the window, "there's something beautiful about seeing the strength of nature displayed like this."

He nodded once in agreement, "some people consider thunderstorms to be violent when in fact they can be really cleansing and rejuvenating. The plants benefit from the water, the dead leaves get blown from the trees, debris and impurities get washed away... not to mention the Selkies and Nymphs in the lakes and rivers draw strength from the water all around them," he turned to look at her, "what were you thinking about before I interrupted you? You looked sad."

"Did I?" she didn't realize until just then that she had felt a bit sad. Well, wistful, really. "I miss my library back home. My grandmother had some amazing books in her collection and on a day like today I could have really lost myself in a good story."

His response was immediate, "we should go to the library in Lark's Valley. I'll take you myself."

She glanced outside once more and back at Rhett, "you want to walk to town right now?"

He chuckled softly, "where did you say you were from? You can't tell me they don't have teleportation portals there."

Attempting to avoid his first question, Cassie tried to sound confident, "I'm sure we do but, I've just never really used one myself. Would you show me how?"

Rhett shook his head, looking at her with disappointment, "you're the oddest little witch I've ever met." He continued to mutter to himself as he walked over to her bedroom door, "nearly nineteen years old and you've never cast a spell, just recently held a sword and made a potion for the first time..."

Cassie was trying to think of a way to defend herself when he grabbed her hand, pulling her over to the bedroom door, he closed his eyes and whispered what Cassie assumed was a spell under his breath. As he spoke, the door knob began to glow in his grasp. The light grew brighter until its radiance cast shadows around the room.

"What did you say?" Cassie asked impatiently. She was tired of everyone muttering spells so quietly that she couldn't hear them.

Rhett looked back at her, his face twisted in confusion, "it's rude to ask someone what they say when the cast their spells." His face softened, "I'm sure that will be part of your lessons with Annie. Now," he began to turn the handle, "have a look."

Beyond the doorway where Cassie would normally expect to see her bed and wardrobe, she instead saw an endless expanse of shelves and desks full of books and aisles full of people, both Fae and human.

"How does this work?" Cassie stepped across the threshold, Rhett closing the door behind them. Cassie turned as the door latched and saw not the hallway they were just in, but the large, glass front doors of the library looking out onto the rainy village street.

"To cast a teleportation spell, you only need one thing: a door. Any door will do no matter where it is as long as you have permission to go through it. I couldn't just teleport into someone's home without first getting permission and, some places like dungeons or banks have portal blocking spells in place so you can't teleport there at all. Public places like this, though, are free reign."

At first, Cassie couldn't make herself take a step forward. The beauty of the familiar—the variety of books, soft murmur of people, the focused look on their faces as they studied the books in their hands— made her heart ache. Along with that ache came a feeling of wonder as she noticed bits of magic dotted here and there, mixed in with the mundane.

She gasped quietly as her eyes traveled upward, seeing the library was without a roof. The ceiling was gone, and although the storm still raged on outside, the droplets of water didn't fall past the upper walls. Instead, it bounced against an unseen barrier, dripping down to the busy street below.

However, there appeared to be a few things that were able to effortlessly come through the magical roof. Little birds, squirrels, bats and even owls dove down from the tree branches overlooking the library, the air only slightly rippling as they passed through the barrier.

She watched one small bluebird come soaring in carelessly, zooming towards one of the impossibly tall shelves. Its intentions soon were made clear as it grasped a book from the highest shelf, the weight of it dragging the bird downward. Its wings struggled to support the extra weight, and it began to plummet.

Cassie took a step forward in shock, but before she knew it, the bird and book had landed safely in the hands of a smiling Fae woman. The bird chirped happily, releasing the book and darting back to the tree above. The woman walked away, opening the book and skimming the first page with eager eyes.

That bluebird wasn't the only one grabbing books. In fact, all of the animals here seemed hard at work. She quickly noticed that all of the books had little handles attached to them to make it easier for the animals to grasp the slippery covers.

"Watch out," Rhett drew her attention back downward just as an owl flew through the air with a heavy-looking tomb, nearly ramming into Cassie's head. She ducked quickly, narrowly avoiding a collision.

Rhett silently led her further into the building, although, Cassie realized there was nothing else silent about this library. In fact, this enormous building seemed to be quite the hub of activity. Conversations buzzed around filling the air with laughter and the drone of multiple voices.

"I thought libraries were supposed to be quiet." Cassie mused.

Rhett pointed to an area in the corner of the room that was marked off by red velvet ropes. There, people curled themselves on comfy looking furniture as they read their books.

"You can be as loud as you want unless you're in the reading area. Over there the area is covered by a soundproof ward, so they can't hear any of this." Rhett waved his hand in the air, referring to the noise around him.

"How do you know so much about libraries?" Cassie casually asked.

Rhett shrugged, "I used to spend a lot of time here as a kid. Didn't have many friends. Except the statues."

Cassie allowed her confusion to show on her face, "statues?" She repeated.

"We preferred to be called Sid."

Cassie jumped as the stone bust to her right spoke, sporting a heavy English accent.

"How are you today, Sid?" Rhett smiled.

"Very well, master Daniels, are you looking for a book in my aisle?"

"Just giving Cass a tour of the library. Not looking for a book today."

They moved onward, passing a variety of statues that stood at the end of every aisle.

Cassie whispered to Rhett in a low voice, "so are they all called Sid?" He nodded and she pointed toward a statue in the form of a voluptuous woman, "even her?"

He chuckled and nodded again, "SID stands for sentient, intelligent directors. Each aisle has a Sid and every Sid knows exactly where each book is in their aisle. They can direct a person or an animal to exactly where the book is that they are looking for."

Just then, a thought floated through her mind, "maybe I should check out a book on spell casting. Just to prepare for Annie's lesson."

Rhett gestured to a broad-shouldered statue, "ask the Sid!"

Uncomfortable and unsure about how to start a conversation with a statue, Cassie slowly approached the Sid.

"Um," she cleared her throat, "hello?"

The Sid turned, his expression blank, bored almost. "Yeah?"

"I'm looking for a book."

"I gathered that." If the statue had arms Cassie bet he would have been crossing them impatiently.

"Spell casting," she blurted, "my first lesson is coming up and..."

The statue whistled sharply, and a squirrel scurried up his back. The statue said something in a low voice and the squirrel hurried away. Cassie stood silently, feeling awkward. She looked back at Rhett who only smiled encouragingly. Moments later the little squirrel was back, dragging a thick, leather bound book across the floor. Cassie met the struggling animal halfway and took the books from its tiny claws.

"Thank you," she whispered to the squirrel as he scampered away once again.

"Easier than you thought, huh?" Rhett said as she made her way back to him. "Wanna get out of here?"

"Don't I have to check this out first?" She gestured to the book in her hand, looking around for a librarian.

"The Sids make note of who takes books. You automatically have them for two weeks, then they come back here."

"They come back? On their own?"

"They're charmed. In exactly two weeks," he flashed his hands open quickly, "poof, they will come back, just like that."

Rhett's eyes wandered around Cassie's face and lit up suddenly, his lips curving into a smile that brought out an endearing dimple in his cheek, "the rain is lightning up out there. We could take a walk and go get some lunch."

Clutching her book tightly to her chest, Cassie couldn't help but smile back. She nodded, "lead the way."

As the rain dissolved into a fine mist and the sun found its way out from behind a curtain of clouds, Cassie began to feel a warmth that she hadn't felt since she came to this magical world. The warmth of a somewhat normal day; visiting the library, getting coffee, enjoying a summer afternoon with someone she might just call a friend. It was the warmth of pure happiness.

The smile on her face slowly fell as she and Rhett saw a crowd forming up ahead. They were loudly cheering and screaming in excitement; each face in the group a Fae citizen. Their heads were skyward, staring at a tall building the western wall of which was covered with a tarp of some kind.

Their cries of joy only grew louder as the tarp was released from one corner, allowing it to fall away revealing a mural that took up the entire side of the building.

The painting was of a beautiful young Faerie woman, tall and lean, depicted in various tones of black and white. Her hair white as the clouds, her eyes as black as obsidian. Her skin, equally as white as her hair, was laced all over with high contrasting black tattoos of leaves and vines. Her dress, an intricate design of black lace, ran across the length of the mural like ink flowing from a spilled jar. Her lips, painted a devilish red, were turned up into a smirk while she stared at an object she clawed in her grasp; A dead lark.

"Is that...?" Cassie whispered over to Rhett.

He stood, grim-faced as he stared over at the growing crowd and the sickening mural. "The Queen." He confirmed her suspicions.

"Why is she painted in black and white while the rest of it's in color?" Cassie wondered aloud.

Rhett answered her rhetorical question, "she's not. That's actually what she looks like."

Cassie realized this was the first time she had seen this elusive Queen. She wasn't sure what she was expecting, but it certainly wasn't this beautiful goddess-like being; so young and striking. She stood, staring for a moment, unable to take her eyes of of the dead bird, knowing it was meant to represent her family.

This painting was more than a way to honor their Queen. This was a statement: Death to the Larkens. With their paint and their shrieks of happiness, the Fae were saying more than words ever could.

"Let's get out of here," Rhett reached over to put his hand on her lower back, leading her away from the energetic crowd, "wouldn't be unusual for this crowd to turn into a mob. Fae can be pretty impulsive when they get excited like that."

He turned the corner and kept his hand firmly in place, hurrying her along. Rhett slowed as Cassie saw an advertisement for "the best coffee in Lark's Valley" on the corner of the street.

Inside the cafe, the pair slid into two of the only empty seats at a high top table in the far corner of the room. The business was simply called "Lark's Valley Cafe" as it read in bold lettering across the front counter. The decor was very minimal, with natural dark wood details and different shades of blue paint. Judging by the long line of customers, the Cafe seemed to be doing a lot of business.

From the table, the two of them studied the menu and Cassie was relieved to find that she was familiar with most of the products available. Among the menu were lattes, cappuccinos, and espresso. Mocha, caramel and cherry were part of the long list of flavor options, as well as a small section of additives written in a metallic, gold ink.

"Charisma shot?" Cassie read one of the golden words aloud, and then another, "Luck?"

Rhett shrugged, "not really my thing, but order it if you'd like. My treat."

Not wanting to seem extremely out of the loop (which she most certainly was) Cassie let the question go, deciding they must just be fun made up words to attract customers.

One Barista called out an order, "tall, decaf, dark roast with extra Calm for Ben!"

Just then, an average yet anxious and uneasy-looking man ran up to the counter and yanked the to-go cup from the Barista's hand, sloshing some of the coffee onto the counter in the process. Eagerly, he took a gulp of the drink as if he were going to die had he went just one more moment without it.

Almost instantaneously, the man's shoulders relaxed and the crazed look faded from his face. Slowly, he lowered the drink from his lips and leaned against the counter for support. He took another sip and suddenly he was sliding down to the floor.

"Jeff!" One barista called to another, "how much Calm did you put in that coffee? This guy's about to take a nap in the middle of the floor!"

Well, Cassie thought, quickly deciding to not order anything from the gold-colored list, *that answers my question; definitely not just funny names.*

Less than ten minutes later, Rhett and Cassie had placed their order, Rhett kindly paying for the meal, and received their food in a most timely manner. Cassie eagerly bit into her savory spinach and feta filled pastry.

"She's beautiful." Cassie said, unable to get the vision of the Fae Queen out of her mind.

"Who?" Rhett looked around, confused.

"The Fae Queen." Her hand drifted absentmindedly to the key she wore around her neck as she did often when thinking of things that troubled her. She twirled the metal, warm from lying against her skin.

Rhett grunted, "I suppose."

The portrait reminded Cassie of a still from an old black and white movie. The Fae Queen was a timeless beauty; a vision in monochrome, haunting and enticing all at once. An image of a fallen angel crept into Cassie's mind, equal parts gorgeous and dangerous.

Rhett clasped his steaming mug of black coffee, staring at her with a smirk. "So," he began, attempting to change the subject, "that night at the bonfire you got to ask me about my family... and my hair. Now it's my turn to ask some questions."

She snorted, tearing off another bite of pastry, "what would you possibly want to know about me?"

"I've been curious," he stared her straight in the eye, "how do you know so little about the world you live in? When I met you in the street that night, you said you had traveled a long way. Where are you from?"

She swallowed hard, racking her brain for an answer. She couldn't be honest with him without revealing who she really was, but was she creative enough to come up with a plausible story? She started down at her mug of chamomile tea, watching the steam rise and fall.

"Can we move on to your next question?" She tried to smile politely while still avoiding eye contact, "it's just that, I come from somewhere that I'm... trying to forget. Emily and I, well, where we come from..." she sighed, "it's really not the best place."

He stared at her with narrowed eyes for a moment, taking the first sip of his drink. "Fair enough," he finally said, though Cassie knew it was just out of politeness, not that he truly accepted that answer. Rhett leaned in closer, "you're gripping that key for dear life. What is it?"

"Oh, uh," she cleared her throat, "it was my grandma's."

"What does it unlock?"

She smiled, remembering when she had, not so long ago, asked herself the same question. How different her life would be now if she had never found the answer! Cassie realized Rhett was still staring at her, expecting a response.

"I never found out," she quickly followed her lie with the truth, "I just wear it to remind me of her. You know?"

Rhett's hand drifted to his wrist. Cassie hadn't noticed the thin leather bracelet tied there. It was nothing more than a strip of worn, brown leather, but Rhett's face told her it was much more to him than a simple scrap of material. She didn't pry, and he didn't offer anything more.

He moved on to his next question, "before you came here and filled your days with training, what did you do for fun?"

Another question about her past. She shrugged off the feeling that this might not be a friendly Q & A but in fact, more of an investigation. She decided to tell the truth while answering this question.

"I liked to bake," she took another bite of pastry, smiling and closing her eyes as she savored the flavor, "but, I don't think I've ever made anything as delicious as this."

"You like to read, too," he offered to further the conversation.

"Yes, books, lots of books. When I wasn't reading or baking, Emily and I spent a lot of time together too, just talking for hours on end," she smiled fondly, "she's like a sister to me."

"But you don't have siblings," he stated, remembering their last conversation.

"No," she said sadly, though now she knew this wasn't exactly true, "my grandmother was my only family."

"Are you having a good time today?" She peered up at him then. He looked hopeful as his grin widened into a full smile.

"Yes." She answered truthfully, without hesitation, "thank you."

"You're welcome, though, *I* should be thanking *you*."

"For what?"

"I'm having a good day too, but you had no reason to want to spend time with me; I wasn't exactly cordial with you when we first met."

"No," she whispered, remembering his cold glare in the hallway that first night and many nights following, "but I understand why. You're just trying to protect the people you care about. There's nothing wrong with that."

He sat, thoughtful for a moment. "Let me take you out again sometime."

Cassie couldn't help but grin, feeling silly when a prickle of excitement ran up her neck at the thought of another day with Rhett.

"Oh?" She said, trying not to let that excitement show, "what would we do?"

"Haven't figured that part out yet," he admitted, "I just know I want to get to know you more."

Cassie hid under her eyelashes, taking a sip of her tea, trying to decide how to respond. "I'd like that." she said, finally.

~ Nine ~

Cassie closed her eyes, listening to the lapping of the waves gently coming ashore as seagulls called overhead. The light breeze blew the salty sea air all around and her bare feet squished in the wet sand while the waves slapped her ankles. Emily lay out silently behind her, soaking in the sun of the beautiful day.

"Cassie," Emily began, sitting up in the sand, "would you come here for a moment?"

Cassie obliged, tearing herself away from the beautiful ocean, going to sit next to her friend. "What's up, Em?"

Emily lowered her borrowed pair of sunglasses, "I wanted to apologize."

"Apologize?" Cassie chuckled, "but you've got nothing to apologize for."

"It's just," Emily's shoulders slouched and she played with the sand at her sides, picking up handfuls and letting them sift through her fingers, "I know I've been spending a lot of time with Annie, and she's really wonderful and I've been having the absolute best time of my whole life here, Cassie... but I know I've been leaving you alone a lot, and I haven't really been the greatest friend. I just wanted to say sorry and—"

"Em," Cassie put a hand on her friend's shoulder, "you really don't have to apologize. I've been having a wonderful time, too. For the most part," she added quietly, "it's slightly stressful being in a magical world I was rescued from as an infant surrounded by family that I need to conceal my identity from or else face a certain death," she smiled sarcastically, "other than that it's been just peachy."

"Cassie, I'm serious," Emily looked forlorn, "I feel like a horrible friend."

"Emily," Cassie said slowly, "you are the best friend anyone could ever ask for. I can't think of a single other person that would have followed me here and stayed by my side, no questions asked. Besides," Cassie scooted closer, whispering, "you hanging out with Annie has given me chance to get to know a certain, handsome, Faerie gentleman a bit better."

"Oh?" this piqued Emily's interest. Her head perked up and her eyes shone with the intrigue that came with hearing potential gossip, "does your gentleman friend also happen to have long, apple-red hair?"

Cassie giggled. She felt silly talking about him like this, as if she and Emily were back in high school, crushing on boys from afar.

"Indeed he does. He took me to the library in town the other day, and afterwards during lunch he told me he wanted to get to know me better."

Emily smiled, but her tone was serious, "as much as I love a good gossip-worthy budding romance, I worry about you going out with him. What if wanting to get to know you better wasn't exactly meant in a friendly way? He could just be suspicious of you and trying to get your secrets out in the open."

Cassie blinked, shocked, "since when are you the logical one? I thought you'd be super excited for me." Her heart sank a bit while the warm flush of embarrassment crept onto her cheeks.

Emily was quiet for a moment, searching Cassie's face for something. Finally she sighed, "I am happy for you if you're happy. I just want you to be careful, that's all," she stood, brushing the sand from her legs and back before extending a hand to Cassie, "come on, maybe Annie can teach you a good self-defense spell during our first lesson today in case Rhett tries anything funny."

"I nearly forgot about that," Cassie took Emily's hand, lifting herself to her feet, "as much as I have enjoyed Grant's lessons, and as rewarding as the training with Vi has been, I think I'm most excited to get into the Spellcraft."

The girls hurried off the beach and back into the Larken's home. As the grandfather clock in the living room chimed twelve times, Cassie hoped Annie wouldn't be upset that they were a minute or two late, for they had been told to meet in Annie's room at noon, exactly.

Upon entering the room, Cassie's first thought was that she had not ever seen so much color all in one place. Tapestries covered the walls, weaved with many different patterns and an array of dyed thread. The tall, four post bed was filled with so many decorative pillows that Cassie wondered how Annie even slept on it at all.

A few more steps forward, and Cassie looked up, marveling at the beautiful mural painted on the ceiling. It depicted a starry sky, complete with connected constellations and a moon as well.

Annie was curled up on the window seat, tending to some plants she had growing there. Upon closer inspection, Cassie saw that they were all little potted succulents. Each of their terracotta homes had been decorated beautifully with detailed paintings. In the middle of each pot, Annie had left enough space open to put names on each plant. It only took Cassie a moment to see that the names on the pots were also the names of all the members of the house.

"What have you got there?" Cassie wondered aloud.

"Oh, just a bit of green magic, nothing much." Annie waved it off as if it were something you might see every day. Cassie supposed if you lived in this world, you probably *would* see that every day.

Cassie couldn't let it go quite yet, "well how does it work?"

Annie smiled lovingly down at her plants, "I've named each plant after each of my friends so I can keep track of you all. If your plant is doing well, you're doing well. I do my best to make sure these little guys have everything they need; plenty of sunlight, fertilizer, water and love. For example," Annie said pointing to a drooping plant near the back, "this one represents a friend of mine back home. She must be sick right now, because so is the plant. But, your plant," she gestured towards a tall, bright green plant in a blue and white striped pot with Cassie's name written on the side, "is doing exceptionally well. Thriving, one might say."

Cassie smiled, "I feel like I'm thriving, ever since we got here."

"That's so wonderful," Annie smiled brightly, "and it will help with today's lesson. You'll need all the energy you can muster to cast a good spell."

"I've been reading a book about spells," Cassie followed Annie over to a long dresser with many drawers, "and it was saying you need different amounts of energy to cast different spells."

"Ooh, got a head start on your lesson, did ya?" Annie chuckled, searching the drawers, "you're correct. To cast a spell you must draw energy from something. A basic rule is that the more energy you have, the stronger the spell will be. It's possible to draw energy from your own spirit but that can be dangerous and downright draining. It is always best to search for something else to draw energy from such as an element, the moon, the sun, a crystal," she plucked two blue stones from one of the drawers, holding them up so that they sparkled in the light, "or a partner who is willing to give you some of their energy. You must never draw energy from an unwilling partner," she continued, grabbing two silver chalices from the top of the dresser and coming to stand in front of Cassie and Emily, "not only is that some of the darkest magic around but it can have detrimental effects on the person that is stealing the energy."

Annie held out the two rough-edged gemstones, each was as large as her closed fist. "I had these sapphires out charging in the energy of the moon all night," she handed a gem and a chalice each to Emily and Cassie, "you will use these to cast your first spell, A simple one, really, your task will be to fill each of these cups with water."

"Heh," Cassie chuckled nervously, "super simple."

"There is no right way to cast a spell," Annie stood tall, clearly proud of her knowledge—as she should be— " and nothing specific that you have to say. Each spell is like..." she moved her eyes skyward, searching for the right word, "a prayer. No one will be the same as the last; each spell will be personal and unique."

Cassie took a seat where Annie had been moments ago near the window. She held the cold, silver chalice in one hand and the heavy, dark stone in the other. Emily simply sat right were she had been standing, looking up at Annie reminding Cassie of the way a small child might sit and stare up at their grade school teacher.

"The first step," Annie had begun to pace the floor as she spoke, "is to concentrate and feel the energy within your source, in this case, it's the sapphire. While holding the sapphire in your hands focus only on the stone. Remember that every object in this universe has its own energy, its own vibrations. Everything exists on a different wavelength than our own; the goal is to make yourself a part of that object's wavelength in order to give it energy or make it's energy a part of your own in order to draw from its power. This is done purely by sheer will. Concentrate. Clear your mind. Feel the magic within the stone."

Annie was silent for a moment, letting her words sink in. She smiled and closed her eyes as she spoke, "once you feel that you have a connection to the energy you are trying to use, say a little spell or a little prayer, and it's as simple as that."

"What do we say, though, exactly?" Emily was staring between the stone and the cup looking as confused as she had back in algebra class.

"Whatever you'd like," Annie replied, "just find the energy, grab a hold of it, and ask it to fill your cup with water."

Everyone was silent then. Cassie stared at the stone in her hand, waiting to feel something. Wait, was that it? No, she was just holding it so tightly that she could feel her own heartbeat through her hands. She set the chalice down and held the sapphire firmly with both hands, gripping it with white knuckles, starting so hard her eyes nearly crossed.

Annie had crossed the room and placed a hand on Cassie's arm, "relax," she instructed, gently removing Cassie's left hand from the stone and putting the chalice back in it. "Loosen your grip," she pulled Cassie's right fingers down and lay her hand flat, balancing the sapphire in the middle of it. "Breathe," Annie demonstrated by taking an exaggerated breath inward and exhaling slowly.

Cassie did as she was told. Much to her frustration, nothing was happening. There was no feeling or energy of any kind.

"I did it!" Emily squealed, breaking Cassie's intense concentration.

Sure enough, Emily's chalice was half full of water. Cassie stared, a little bit shocked, a little bit more proud of her friend, but mostly annoyed that Emily had figured it out so quickly while Cassie had been struggling.

Annie praised her good work, and turned to Cassie, "did you find the energy yet, Cassidy?"

Cassie did her best to not show her annoyance, "not yet," she set the sapphire down and stood from her seat, "maybe I'll have more luck with the next lesson."

"Sorry, Cassidy," Annie frowned, "but you've got to complete one task before moving to the next."

She gritted her teeth before forcing a smile. She sat back down, taking the stone in her hands once again. She stared at it, her frustration growing. Grandma Charlotte *had* always said Cassie gave up on things too quickly if she wasn't good at it right away.

And so what if that were true? Maybe Spellcasting just wasn't meant to be part of Cassie's skill set. She had picked up on Alchemy right away. And after she had built up the muscle strength, sword fighting had come easily enough as well. What was it about this stone that was baffling her so much?

"I just don't... feel anything." She admitted, huffing out an annoyed breath of air.

"Don't worry," Annie assured her, "everyone learns at their own pace. It doesn't shock me though, that this isn't coming quickly for you."

"What's that supposed to mean?" Cassie's annoyance slowly blossoming into anger.

"Well you were so good with potions and swords," Annie echoed her thoughts, "and those aren't very spiritual practices, they are more step by step, physical arts. While there is some spirituality involved in Alchemy, it is still possible to create a potion without it. Maybe you have a block."

"A block?" Cassie stood up, one of her eyebrows raised questioningly.

"Yes, your spirit might be troubled. Negative energy could prevent you from being able to access your ability to cast spells."

"What should I do about it then?"

"Are you stressed?"

Cassie scoffed, "aren't we all a bit stressed? Preparing for a war?"

"Not at all," Annie said calmly, " I'm confident in our purpose and in myself. No need to be stressed."

Cassie stood, wordlessly, unsure of what to do next. Tears threatened to spill onto her cheeks, as they often did hen she was frustrated. She prayed her voice wouldn't break when she spoke, "I think I just need a minute alone."

Sapphire and chalice still in hand, Cassie walked past the other girls, ignoring Emily as she called out her name. She walked, shoulders hunched, back to her room. Upon passing the stairs, she saw Rhett halfway up them and headed her way.

"Cassie," he smiled for a moment and then the smile fell away upon seeing the tears that had inevitably fallen from her eyes, "what's wrong?"

Cassie only picked up her pace, closing the door of her bedroom behind her as Rhett turned at the top of the stairs to follow her.

She threw herself onto her bed, the chalice and sapphire falling onto the covers next to her. Wrapping her arms around a pillow, she sobbed, allowing the floodgates of emotion to finally open for the first time since coming here.

These tears weren't just from the frustration of not being able to cast a spell on her first try—that would be a bit excessive. No, in fact, she knew these tears weren't for any one thing in particular.

With each sob and each tear, a little of Cassie's anger slipped out. Anger for the secrets her grandma kept from her and anger for having her family so close and yet still out of grasp.

Along with the anger came fear and stress and worry; fear of being alone in a strange place, stress of lying about who she was, and worry that she wasn't lying well enough. And, thrown into the mixture for good measure were overwhelming bits of despair and confusion.

She was a mess, and she had been holding it all in this whole time. Distracting herself with training and focusing on learning as much as she could retain was only going to work for so long, she knew, but what else could she do? It all felt like too much. Too much for one person to handle alone.

She heard voices outside her bedroom door, Rhett and Emily's. A moment later the door clicked open, and Cassie wiped her face in the pillow though she knew it was pointless to try to hide the fact that she'd been crying. She sat up expecting Emily's concerned face and found Rhett's instead.

Surprised and a bit embarrassed, she buried her face in the pillow again. "Go away," she said listlessly, feeling like a child.

Gentle and calloused hands wrapped around Cassie's wrists, slowly pulling them down. She didn't fight him, only stared back with swollen eyes.

"What's wrong?" He whispered.

"I don't even know," she sniffled, "I'm feeling pretty... overwhelmed."

"Do you want to talk about it?"

She shook her head.

"Okay. Can I sit with you?"

After a moment's hesitation she nodded, scooting back to allow him more room on the bed. He quietly lifted himself up, taking her discarded chalice and sapphire into his hands.

Cassie focused on breathing, trying to regain a sense of calm. "Do you feel it?" She asked, her voice muffled by her stuffy nose.

"Feel what?"

"The energy. In the stone."

"Yes. Don't you?"

She shook her head again, fresh tears blurring her vision.

"Here," Rhett scooted closer, holding out the hand that held the sapphire, "put your hand on here."

She listened to his direction. He then placed his other hand on top of hers, holding it in place against the sapphire. "Close your eyes." Again, she listened.

"Sapphires have similar energies to that of water," he explained softly, "It comes in waves; a tingle of cold that washes over your hands and falls away just as quickly. Concentrate on feeling it rise and fall, like the ocean outside. It almost feels like, a vibration, coming from deep within the stone."

Cassie gasped. Her eyes flew open and she pulled her hand back. She was shocked to feel a rumbling coming up from the stone and through her palm. She smiled in delight.

"Did you feel it?" Rhett smiled, too.

"I think so," she said, taking the stone from Rhett's hand. Sure enough, there it was again; a vibration as Rhett had said, buzzing strong and then weakening before growing in strength again and shrinking away, just like the waves crashing against her ankles earlier.

"Yeah, I feel it!"

"Good," he grabbed the chalice and held it out to her, "now focus on the pattern of the vibration, and while focusing, cast your spell."

Excited, Cassie closed her eyes and whispered a small prayer—to whom, she wasn't sure—asking that the cup be filled with water.

"Please..." she added at the end, just in case.

She opened her eyes and laughed happily upon seeing the chalice filled with water.

"I did that?"

"You did," Rhett assured her.

She set down the sapphire and wiped the remaining tears from her face with her sleeve, "thank you."

"My pleasure," Rhett replied, rising from his seat on the bed, "just remember to breathe," he took an exaggerated breath in and out, "and the rest will come naturally."

~ Ten ~

Staring into her open wardrobe full of borrowed clothes was starting to feel more like staring under the hood of a car; Cassie was equally as clueless about fashion as she was about mechanics. However, at this point, attempting to fix a car would be far less intimidating.

Tonight was the night Cassie and Rhett finally got to go on their date. It had been two weeks since he had helped her cast her first spell, and although they had hoped to spend some time together sooner, Rhett had been busy training some new recruits.

Cassie wasn't entirely sure what he had planned for tonight, but even if she had a detailed itinerary with diagrams and bullet points and illustrations, she would still have no clue what to wear.

It was a chilly night so a sweater seemed practical, and Emily had always told her you can never go wrong with a good pair of jeans. Cassie decided to no longer drag out the process of picking out clothes, and grabbed a gray cashmere sweater from the hanger pairing it with deep navy skinny jeans and black suede boots.

Her auburn hair fell in voluminous waves that Emily had helped create earlier in the evening. Cassie wished Emily were here now, to calm her anxiety about tonight, but Emily had planned more spell casting lessons with Annie tonight instead.

Apparently Emily's lessons had been going well, but Cassie had stopped attending them. After their first failed interaction, Cassie had tried to swallow her pride and go back for a few more lessons. While Annie was a kind girl, and passionate, too, she and Cassie were just not compatible when it came to having a student-teacher relationship.

Spellcasting just came so naturally to Annie that she had a hard time explaining the craft to someone like Cassie who needed a bit more direction and patience.

Instead, Cassie had found every book available to her on the subject of Spellcasting and so far teaching herself had been going surprisingly well. She had focused on learning mostly offensive spells, thinking they would be the most useful given the current circumstance. There had been rumors that the Faeries had been planning an ambush on the rebel fighters, and trusted informants warned it would be coming soon.

After sleepless nights full of studying and practicing, Cassie was proud of the little fireball she could produce in the palm of her hand. She could even fill her bathtub with water and conjure a breeze strong enough to whip her hair around and send papers flying throughout the room.

She had used her new-found powers for practical reasons, too, like keeping a mug of tea at the perfect temperature or brightening a dark room with a snap of her fingers.

Of course, with all of this practicing, Cassie quickly learned just how fast one's energy reserves could be depleted. After a few times of passing out from pure exhaustion, she had dedicated a full day to procuring another, more easily recharged energy source in the form of gemstones. Cassie had taken to wearing these gemstones in the most convenient way possible: jewelry.

Cassie had never been one for wearing flashy accessories, but somehow, wearing gemstones as an energy source felt as important as drinking water—a necessary part of her daily routine. She could feel the energy surrounding her as she slipped rings on every other finger, latched a choker adorned with stones around her neck, and placed gemstone studs in her earlobes—all yellow topaz, of course. Even the swords and shields here had gemstones embedded in their hilts and handles, in case the user needed to cast an in-the-moment spell for greater strength or agility.

Cassie took one last look at herself in the full-length mirror and, pleased with her appearance, headed for the door. She stopped just as she was about to turn the handle, remembering she had forgotten one last piece of her wardrobe. Well, she supposed it wasn't so much an accessory as a tool, but nonetheless essential. She grabbed a small iron dagger off the bedside dresser and shoved it safely into her boot, tucking the ruby studded hilt under her pant leg. Not that Cassie expected to need a weapon on her date—if they were to encounter any kind of danger Cassie was sure Rhett would take care of it—but carrying a weapon around, no matter how small, gave her a bit more peace of mind now that she knew how to use one.

Swinging the door open, she bounded out into the hallway, not paying enough attention to notice Rhett was already waiting for her there. She slammed into his chest, but he stood steady, holding her by her upper arms to prevent her from falling over.

"Easy there," he chuckled, but there was something off about his tone.

Cassie looked up, seeing a disappointed look on Rhett's handsome features, "is everything okay?

He took a deep breath, letting it out slowly before answering, giving her enough time to notice he was dressed in the light leather armor the Larkens gave all of their supporters. His beautiful red hair was back in a small, tight bun the way he wore it for training sessions and a glint of annoyance flashed in his emerald eyes. She already knew their date was canceled before he spoke.

Rhett reached his hand up and behind him, rubbing his neck, "there's been an emergency meeting called. Our date's going to have to happen another night, I'm sorry."

A twinge of disappointment fell over Cassie like a frozen blanket but she tried to sound nonchalant, "no worries, let me get changed quickly and we can walk together to the meeting."

He smiled and nodded quickly before she ducked in the bedroom to exchange her casual clothes for armor identical to Rhett's and put her hair up in a high pony tail. She kept the dagger tucked into her boots and decided her jewelry was best kept in place. Part of her was relieved to know exactly what to wear for an occasion like this. She had grown to feel comfortable in her armor and wore it like a second skin.

Cassie was gone less than two minutes, and rushed back out to Rhett who wasted no time hurrying down the hall, out the front door, down the hill, through the Cloaked Door and into the cavern brightened by orange gemstones—the first place he had taken her and Emily when they first arrived in Lark's Valley.

The room was filled once again with rebels here to support the Larkens. Each person was wearing the dark brown leather armor studded in strategic places by iron embedded with bright topaz—yellow and brown were the colors of the Larken family, after all.

Near the front of the crowd, weapons and supplies were being handed out. The rebels grabbed iron swords and iron-tipped arrows made of rowan wood, sliding them into sheaths and filling their quivers before moving on to the next station. There, a few women of the cause, including Lysette, blessed and anointed the soldiers and their weapons. She saw Grant's face in the crowd as well, supplying individuals with his potions.

Charles spoke, with Divina by his side, both looking strong and deadly in full battle gear, "for those of you just arriving, prepare yourselves for a raid larger than we have ever attempted before! Tonight, near one of the castle outposts, a shipment of Xirilium will arrive. Enough Xirilium to supply the entire Faerie army with Xirilium swords and still have a reserve available to stock their armory. We cannot let this shipment reach its destination. Plus," his expression was alight with excitement, "think of the advantage we could have with all of that Xirilium to make weapons of our own! This is an opportunity we cannot let pass us by. Tonight we turn the tide. Tonight," his voice rose louder, "the Larkens will be one step closer to being back on the throne of Lark's Valley— where we belong!"

The crowd erupted with cheers of agreement. Cassie turned to Rhett, "what is Xirilium?"

"It's a rare ore, only mined two months out of the year, because during the other ten months, the mines are flooded and impossible to reach. Faeries use Xirilium to make their weapons and it is the only thing more deadly to Fae than iron or rowan wood," he scoffed, "leave it to the Fae to create a weapon strong enough to take out their entire population."

"If it's so deadly to them, why do they choose to use it?" She wondered aloud.

Rhett continued to explain as they made their way to the front of the room, "Xirilium is one of the purest forms of magical energy. The Fae use it to cast some of the most powerful spells. They outsource it's production of course—if it touches their skin they'll get badly burned—and they make sure the handles are made of wood or steel or any other material, really."

They had reached the supply line. Cassie held out her hand to receive a sword. Rhett swung his arm out, grabbing her by the wrist.

"What are you doing?"

Confused, Cassie looked from Rhett to the sword and back again, "well I can't fight in a raid without a weapon."

Rhett's eyes were fierce with an emotion she hadn't seen him wear before, "you won't be going, Cass. It's too dangerous."

She yanked her wrist back, holding eye contact and defiantly grabbing a sword anyways, "I've been training for this, and I'll be going to do my part just like everyone else here, Rhett. I appreciate your concern," she tried to calm herself—people telling her what she could or couldn't do was the thing she hated most—and softened her tone, "but I can't just stay home and do nothing. Besides," she slid the sword into a sheath at her side, "going on a raid-date with you is better than no date at all, right?"

Rhett's expression told Cassie he didn't agree, but he didn't get a chance to protest before Vi and Grant popped up next to them. Grant took the liberty of stuffing small, one-dose vials of potion into Cassie's empty pockets.

"For strength," he said as he tucked a bright red one in, "endurance," a blueish-green liquid-filled vial went in the other pocket, "and luck," he smiled kindly before handing her and Rhett both an uncorked, cylindrical vial containing a luminescent, neon green potion, "down the hatch!"

"Cheers," Cassie smiled mockingly at Rhett who glared at her as he threw back the potion.

Vi, with her hair braided back loosely and a calm smile on her lips, turned to Rhett and Cassie, "you two can come with me and my crew," she nodded to three strong and confident soldiers murmuring in the corner, "we'll go in first, to clear the way and let the rest know when it's safe to follow."

"Vi," Rhett's voice was low and pleading, "is Cassie really ready for this? Surely she could be on the return team; she would be a great healer."

"Nonsense," the authority in Vi 's voice was clear, "I trained her myself. She's ready."

A surge of pride rose in Cassie's chest. She had been working hard and diligently on her training, and it was satisfying enough to see her efforts paying off let alone being recognized by someone as skilled as Vi.

For a moment, Cassie stared at the girl in front of her, wishing she could tell her the truth about the relationship Vi didn't know they shared. Cassie longed for the chance to tell Vi they were sisters, in hopes that their bond would only be strengthened. However, the longing was soon replaced by a solid survival instinct telling her to keep quiet. Vi had said it herself, if she ever found her sister, she'd have to kill her. End of story.

Cassie tried to distract her thoughts by looking around the room for Emily and Annie, spotting them in the blessing and anointment line. Emily smiled as she spoke a blessing over one brown-haired boy's sword, Annie by her side doing the same thing.

"I'll be right back," Cassie called to Vi and Rhett while Grant scurried into the crowd to distribute more potions.

Rhett refused to look at her, but Vi nodded, "meet back here in five."

Cassie rushed over, pushing her way through the crowd to get to her friend. "Emily!" She called.

At the sound of Cassie's voice, Emily's head jerked up, and she smiled brightly. "Cassie," Emily sighed with relief as Cassie got

closer, "this place is a madhouse. Look at you!" Emily laughed in disbelief, "all dressed up like a proper soldier! Here," she said, placing one hand on the hilt of Cassie's sword and the other on Cassie's
shoulder. She closed her eyes and said a quick blessing before wrapping her arms around Cassie in a tight hug, "be safe out there
tonight."

Tears nearly welled up in Cassie's eyes but she clenched them
tightly shut. "Of course. I'll see you soon. I just wanted to come say
goodbye but I've gotta go; Vi, Rhett and the others are waiting for
me."

"I'll see you later." Emily's words came out more like a demand
than a simple statement, making Cassie smile.

A minute later Cassie was outside with Rhett, Vi and "the crew"
as Vi had called them. Cassie had seen the three of them in trainings
or moving about the Larken's home occasionally, but knew little of
them besides their names.

The oldest among them, Xavier, was tall and stoic with a weathered face and graying hair. Cassie hadn't heard him talk much, but
his mastery of sword fighting said more about him than words ever
could.

Johanna—or Jo for short—managed a smirk at Cassie when she
approached, and that was the most emotion Cassie had ever seen
from the broad-shouldered woman with deep black hair that rose in
short spikes from her head.

The youngest of the group—a boy Cassie had heard called Jimmy,
which she assumed was short for James—stood wide eyed and anxious on the outer edge of the group. This surprised Cassie, as he was
always the most loud and boastful of the group, constantly talking
about how he was ready to cut down any Faerie in his path. "The Fae

will rue the day they were born if they ever find themselves on the other end of my sword," he'd say consistently.

The sun was setting over the ocean and the sky was bursting with pinks, oranges and purples that were mirrored perfectly by the deep waters. Now, as reality began to sink in, Cassie wondered if this would be the last sunset she might ever see.

I wonder if dying will be painful, the thought floated through her mind as errant as a thought one might have when remembering an item to add to their grocery list. It was there and then it was gone, and Cassie thought of Rhett then, his anger and concern coming to the forefront of her mind.

"Alright team, let's head out. The outpost isn't far from here. Keep up," Vi broke into a light jog and headed down the beach, towards the castle.

Rhett brought up the rear of the group, and Cassie adjusted her pace to meet his, "Rhett," she whispered, but wasn't sure what else to say.

He didn't respond right away, but he did look over at her, his eyes soft. Quietly, he said, "just, don't take any unnecessary risks, and stay close to me. Please."

That she could agree to. She smiled back at him before dropping her voice low, anxiety overwhelming her momentary sense of relief, "I've never killed anyone, Rhett."

The group had slowed their pace as they reached the outer edge of the town wall. Slowly they walked along the wall, trying to maintain their stealth. Their destination, a tall and wide structure with a pair of even taller watch towers on either side, was only about a quarter mile away on the western edge of the castle.

Rhett spared a moment to turn and take Cassie's hands, "you can turn back now and you won't have to. I won't judge you for choosing that. Killing people— even the Fae— is something you'll live with for the rest of your life."

Cassie swallowed hard, but she had already made her choice to fight and was going to stand by that. "I can do this."

Rhett squeezed her hand and smiled slightly, "I know you can. We're doing the right thing here, Cassie. It can help a bit if you remember that. Remember that unfortunate couple in the street that day. Remember the Fae guards who did nothing. You're fighting for the freedom of your people. There is no greater honor than that."

Vi raised a fist, signaling for them to stop. They had come to a group of tall bushes, thick with greenery, that continued along the wall and out into the field. Vi nodded, keeping her eyes on the sentry atop the tower, and Jo darted into the bushes, drawing her bow and knocking an arrow back. She let it fly and then repeated the motion a second time.

Only a moment later the Fae guards grunted, an arrow protruding from each of their chests. They began to fall forward, toppling over the edge. Before the bodies hit the ground, Xavier jumped into action, casting a spell that slowed the soldier's momentum, allowing their bodies to fall to the ground without a sound.

The group didn't waste a second, rushing into the field and over to the now-empty guard tower. For the moment they were out in the open, Cassie squirmed inside at the thought of being so painfully exposed with no cover whatsoever. She found herself drawing energy from one of her rings to cast a small spell asking for her group to be soundless, hoping to conceal at least their noise if not the sight of them.

Whether it helped or not, Cassie wasn't sure, but she was pleased to find that as they scaled the stone tower, their boots and hooks made absolutely no sound. Surely, this would help them maintain the element of surprise.

Once atop the tower, Cassie saw that a walkway ran behind the main building connecting the two sentry posts. At the moment, there didn't appear to be anyone on the other side. The five of them didn't wait for someone to show up. They rushed across the walkway and ducked under the cover of the other tower's roof.

This watch tower was connected to the building below by a set of spiral stairs that went downward from the center of the tower. A moment after discovering the stairs, two guards appeared at the top of them.

Rhett and Vi broke away from the group in an instant. The guards didn't even have a moment to register the situation before Rhett and Vi were on them. Vi's sword came down hard on the helmet of one soldier. She plunged the tip of it deep into his chest as he fell to his knees. Rhett had jumped the other soldier from behind, taking a dagger that had been concealed in his sleeve and slitting the guard's throat. The two Fae soldiers fell into pools of their own blood.

Cassie's knees began to tremble and her mouth ran dry. It wasn't the death or the brutal delivery of it that was nauseating her. It was the blood itself that sickened her, and not simply for being blood, but for the small fact of it being red.

These Fae men bled just the same as she did from hearts that pumped in their chests same as her own. Bright red blood flowed from their wounds as they died for a cause not so different than hers. They too wanted their people to rule just as Cassie wanted her family to.

There was no more time to linger on the thought. Jimmy, who up until this point had been silently at her side, stood by the far wall of the tower, lifting his hand and producing a flame that flickered thrice, growing bright and dim in a steady on and off pattern.

It was then that Cassie saw them; the rest of the rebel forces waiting in the trees of a small patch of forest a half mile or so away. They were shrouded in the growing shadows of the setting sun, but sent back a small flare as well to show they had received the signal.

"We don't know how many are in there," Vi was breathing heavily, the rush of the moment spiking her adrenaline, "we have to go in, so keep yourselves on high alert. Remember, we aren't trying to win, we're creating the distraction. My father and the others will bust in to help us and bring the extraction team. Just try to stay alive."

Cassie's arm shook with fear and excitement as she reached for the sword at her side. The weight of the metal in her grasp steadied her for a moment. She took a deep breath, and prayed she would stay level-headed in the inevitable fight that she knew she would soon find herself in the middle of.

In a single-file line, they moved down the stairs. Vi peered around the corner once she reached the bottom and signaled the coast was clear. The five of them filled the small corridor at the bottom of the staircase. She could hear voices coming from beyond the doorway in front of them, but just how many were there she wasn't sure.

Xavier approached the door and placed his hand flat upon the wood, charming the door to be like one way glass, giving them the advantage of seeing beyond it while still being concealed behind it.

In the room on the other side of the door, a giant block of what could only be the Xirilium shipment sat in the middle of the room, strapped to a series of wheeled carts. Cassie stifled a gasp at the Xirilium's brilliance. It was solid and thick, with a slight translucency that wasn't clear enough to see through to the other side, but to see a few feet inside the block of stone. The Xirilium was a deep burgundy with swirls of maroon and red strewn throughout.

From where they sat, only five guards were visible; an even fight. Xaviar looked back at Vi who nodded once. Xaviar kicked in the door, rushing into the room with a battle cry. Vi and Jo followed suit screaming at the top of their lungs. Jimmy and Rhett ran in next, swords drawn and Cassie followed close behind, taking inventory of the scene playing out in front of her.

Vi was in a heated battle with two Fae guards, but she was smiling brightly as she fended them off. To her right, Xaviar took on the biggest guard on the floor, and appeared to be equally matched.

The sound of the rebel's iron clanging off of the Fae's Xirilium swords filled the air as Jo launched herself onto a stack of barrels. Using her bow, she managed to pick off guards stationed on the upper floor before they could make their way down the stairs.

A ball of fire flew from Jimmy's hands, a look of focus on his face as he advanced on the guard in front of him. The only other guard on the floor was being furiously attacked by Rhett. He was steadily taking steps forward while slicing his sword through the air, the Fae soldier struggling to defend against Rhett's unyielding attacks.

Still awkwardly in the doorway without an opponent, Cassie scanned the room. The main door was banging, the reinforcements trying to break their way in but struggling to bust through a thick metal beam that fell across the middle of the thick wooden door.

Cassie sprung from her spot, dodging the battles ensuing before her. She made her way to the door, trying to shove the metal bar up and out of its resting place. It wasn't budging. She cast a spell to propel the bar upward, which helped but still didn't remove it from the latch.

She looked around the room. More guards had emerged from the upper and lower levels of the building. Vi's smile had vanished as she fended off four opponents and Jimmy was looking exhausted, his fireballs burning a little smaller than they had initially.

Rhett had defeated his guard who lay in a crumpled pile on the ground. Cassie had lost sight of Jo and Xaviar, and knew the rest of the team needed to get inside. Now.

Letting out a frustrated scream, she retrieved Grant's potions from her pocket, biting the corks and spitting them out onto the ground. She downed the contents of the vials without even tasting them.

A surge of energy flowed through her the moment the potions hit her stomach. She could feel it building in intensity, the power shaking her vision and making her knees wobble. As the power within her peaked, she focused all of her strength into her arms, and shoved with all of her might on the bolt.

It flew into the air and landed on a pair of guards that had been advancing on Xaviar. He jumped back in surprise, looked over at her, and cheered as the reinforcements burst through the door.

Rhett cut down another Fae man, then turned his attention to the door, catching sight of Cassie. He smiled and started to walk toward her but Cassie was already on the move.

"Rhett!" She screamed, her sight focused on the massive Faerie man with an equally oversized Xirilium axe headed for Rhett from behind. Axe raised, the Faerie man screamed.

Rhett spun, barely raising his sword in enough time to block the attack. He fell to the floor, staring up at the Fae man who was already on the downswing of his next attack.

Cassie launched herself into the air, closing the last of the short distance between herself and Rhett's attacker. The potions weren't supposed to give her courage as well, but Cassie felt entirely confident as she attached herself to his torso. She was close enough to smell the rot of old meat on his breath, but it didn't faze her.

She only had an instant of his shock to react. Dagger in hand, she thrust it into the soldier's neck and shoved her way off of him, falling not-so-gracefully onto her back next to Rhett.

Blood spurted from the wound and the soldier staggered backward once, before falling forward. Rhett rolled, gathering Cassie in his arms. He rolled once more, moving them only inches out of the way; the soldier's heavy body slamming to the ground where Cassie had been only moments before.

A rumbling drew their attention to the pile of Xirilium in the center of the room. The battle around them slowed and then stopped altogether when the surviving Fae soldiers suddenly vanished, leaving behind only a cloud of smoke where they once stood.

"This isn't good." Rhett pulled Cassie to her feet.

Charles's voice boomed over the crowd, "retreat!"

The rumbling intensified to the point of making Cassie stumble. A crack appeared in the block of Xirilium and another, and another. Rhett and Cassie were as far from the door as one could get in that building. They broke into a run a second too late.

The Xirilium exploded from within, fiery hunks of heavy stone flew around the room. One moment the crowd was hustling towards the door and the next bodies were falling all around them.

A shadow fell over them. Cassie looked up, a piece of rubble was seconds away from falling on her. She skidded out of the way. A wave of pain shot up her leg as she landed on her foot wrong. She fell to the ground, calling out for Rhett.

They met eyes and the strangest sensation shot through her body. Every atom in her body vibrated, as if she were being painlessly electrocuted, and every hair on her skin stood straight up.

Cassie was suddenly very aware of every source of energy around her, the most overwhelming of them all, Rhett, who was standing only inches away from her.

The room around them went silent. The lights dimmed and Cassie looked around, bewildered. Everything besides the two of them was moving in slow motion. Was this shock? A crazy side effect of the potions? An adrenaline rush?

"Cassidy," Rhett spoke at normal speed as the world blurred around them, "what are you doing?"

"I— I'm doing this?"

"You've... slowed time," he fell to his knees, "and you're using my energy to do it."

"How do I stop?" She asked, frantic and starting to panic.

Rhett had taken his endurance potion Grant had gave him and jumped to his feet. "I have no idea," he hooked his arms around her, lifting her from the ground and heading for the exit, "but keep it up for just a moment more."

Two steps out of the door, time began to speed up again. Rhett and Cassie, along with the other survivors, collapsed on the ground outside the blazing building.

The heat from the inferno was nearly choking her as Cassie scrambled backwards, one leg dragging uselessly behind her, trying to put distance between herself and the flames. Once she and Rhett were far enough away, lying on the ground next to each other, she turned to him, gasping for air.

"Rhett...I...don't under...stand."

Rhett lay, staring up at the stars, slowly shaking his head in disbelief, "I don't either," he rolled to his side, "what we just did in there, our energies, together...that was... Cassie?"

Slowly, Cassie begun to feel a coldness creep over her body. She was still gasping for breath, and no longer noticed the pain in her leg. Her eyes fluttered closed and she welcomed the calm feeling that came over her.

She was vaguely aware of Rhett's voice calling her name. Her eyes focused on the silhouette of his head against the full moon above as unconsciousness claimed her.

~ Eleven ~

Cassie knew she was awake, but didn't want to open her eyes quite yet. The last thing she remembered was lying on the cold ground with Rhett after the failed raid. She didn't feel like she was on the cold, hard ground anymore, but she has no idea where she was.

Slowly, she took inventory of her body. She wiggled her toes—all present. Her left leg felt fine but the right one was quite sore. She winced but continued on with her inspection, finding no pain in her gut or torso. Eyes, ears, mouth, nose, all in the correct place. When she wiggled her fingers, she heard a chair scoot backward, and steps coming towards her.

She froze, eyes still closed, as a hand brushed hair from her forehead. "I told you that you should have stayed home." Rhett's tone was meant to be teasing but only sounded relieved.

Now, Cassie felt a smile creep onto her lips. She allowed her eyes to slowly flutter open as she spoke softly, "if I had stayed home you'd have an axe in your back or be burned alive."

He chuckled humorlessly, "I suppose you're not wrong. I'm just glad you're not more seriously hurt."

She realized then that they were in her room back at the Larken's home and she was in pajamas, tucked into bed with a pillow propping her right leg up. She moved to sit up more, and Rhett rushed to support her.

"It's already looking a little less swollen." Rhett commented, nodding toward her leg, "when we got back, Annie and Emily took care of the bone and Grant sped up the healing with a potion, but it only works in doses. Here," he reached over to take a steaming mug off of the nightstand, "I mixed the last dose into this, but don't worry, it's tasteless."

As she took the warm porcelain her hands, she recognized the unmistakable scent of her favorite tea. "Chamomile?" She couldn't help but sound shocked.

He shrugged, "Emily told me it was your favorite."

She thanked him as she tightened her grip on the mug, feeling the heat seep into her skin. Cassie held it near her nose, letting the aroma fill her face before taking a sip.

"What happened to the Xirilium?" She asked, her memory coming back to her.

"It's all gone," he nearly growled, " The Fae sabotaged it all in an attempt to wipe us out."

A wave of disappointment hit her followed by an even greater wave of anxiety as she remembered seeing bodies falling around her, "Did Vi make it out? Jimmy? Charles?"

"Relax," Rhett placed his hand on hers, "they're fine." His expression told her that someone else hadn't been as lucky.

"Who?" She spoke quietly.

Rhett paused, "we took a hit. Sustained a lot of loss. Jo and Xavier being two of the many."

"Oh." She said in a small voice.

Cassie wouldn't cry for them; no, they died an honorable death. They died for what they believed in and their sacrifice would certainly not be in vain, but the sadness she felt was still achingly real.

"We'll have a memorial for them. But," he paused, searching her features with tired eyes, "Cassie, listen," Rhett began again, slowly changing the subject, "there's something I need to talk to you about. Tonight was really..." He pursed his lips, trying to find the words.

"Scary." Cassie whispered.

"A little," he admitted with a grin. "But, to think we were so easily fooled— we knew an ambush was coming but... how could we be so naïve? There's got to be a spy among us, Cassie, and..." he looked into her eyes with a deep sadness, "the others are whispering. Wondering if... you and Emily aren't..."

Cassie nearly choked on her tea, "what? Spies? How could anyone think that? I almost died in there along with everyone else!"

Rhett looked pained, "I know it's not true."

"But?" Cassie prompted.

"Trust me, after that spell you cast earlier with my energy... Cass, that was advanced magic. Partners who practice together for years couldn't even pull that off." He shook his head in disbelief, "for it to have been successful means there's an undeniable connection between us."

"What's your point?" Cassie chirped, not unkindly but with a certain undertone of impatience.

Rhett seemed to be unaware of her growing annoyance, "I think it's because of that connection that I can just feel it. You're not the spy, you can't be."

"How do we convince the others?" She tried to ignore the pounding of her frantic heart when he admitted to feeling that same connection she felt; like the overwhelming feeling that washed over her back in the outpost. That moment when his energy was so easily accessible, so tantalizing, so irresistible, it felt as if he wanted her to take it; like he was giving it away so willingly.

"There may not be a way to convince them of anything. The best way is to find the real spy and get them out into the open."

"How do we do that?"

"Your guess is as good as mine."

She scoffed unattractively, "why Emily and I? What did we do to become suspicious? We've done nothing but dedicate ourselves to this place, to this fight."

He shrugged, "truth is, it's just because you're the newest ones here. No one really knows anything about you or Emily, and when a mind is left to come to its own conclusions, it's not hard for things to get a little crazy."

"Rhett, I—" tears of frustration began to fill her eyes. She wanted so badly to admit the truth to him, but how could she afford to? Throughout her time here, she'd been so careful about keeping her identity hidden, but the question now was whether it was better to reveal who she was or let them think she was a spy for the Fae Queen. "I cant tell you what you want to hear."

He was quiet for a moment. His eyes continued flickering around, searching her face for an answer he wouldn't find. Finally he took her hand, "I wont make you do or say anything that makes you uncomfortable. But," he tightened his grip, "if I take your side, and assure everyone you're truly with us for the long haul, then I just ask you don't make me a liar."

She squeezed his hand in return and nodded her head, unsure what to say next. She wiped the tears from her eyes, forcing a smile, "I won't."

He grinned, his thumb gently rubbing back and forth on her palm, "enough of this," his voice livened, "I was going to wait to ask you this until after our date, but obviously that never happened. What I wanted to say was that I think you need to come with me tomorrow, if you're feeling better of course."

"Come with you?"

"I'm going to see my aunt, my only surviving Fae relative, and I want you to meet her. I also have some leads to follow up on in the Faerie village about the ambush but, either way, I'd like you to come with me."

"You want to take me to a Faerie village? The day after a raid? That sounds... dangerous." She couldn't hide the shock in her voice.

He smiled brightly, "you'll be safe with me. Besides, if you wear the right outfit, no one will be able to tell you're human at first glance." His eyes glistened with excitement, "so was that a yes?"

A nervous giggle escaped her lips as exhaustion crept up on her again, "that depends, is your aunt a nice lady?"

He chuckled, "well, *I* think so."

He stood to leave and Cassie settled back into her blankets, "finish your tea and get some rest," he instructed, "oh and, I almost forgot: Emily said she's going to check in on you tonight, but she's still tending to the other injured."

Cassie reluctantly pulled her hand out of his, "thank you, Rhett."

She watched with a sleepy smile on her face while he left the room. When the door clicked shut though, she released the breath she hadn't realized she was holding, and sighed.

What was she doing? *I didn't come here for love,* she reminded herself halfheartedly, *I have to keep my eye on the end goal—helping my family.*

Her hand was still warm from his grasp and it felt as though the heat were radiating through her body, burning away the twinge of guilt and uncertainty she had begun to feel. Cassie was thankful when her eyelids became heavy just then, and she knew sleep was not far away.

She burrowed under the covers telling herself that tonight she wouldn't worry about what happens next. No, tonight Cassie wouldn't be a Lost Princess fighting Faeries in a dangerous, magical world. For now she was simply Cassie Larken, and she was hanging on to every little bit of happiness that his warmth brought her.

~ Twelve ~

Despite being exhausted from the long night, Cassie had eagerly jumped out of bed that morning excited to go on this day trip with Rhett. However, now that she and Rhett were standing at the entrance of the forest of the Fae, she was beginning to feel a bit drained again.

Rhett had led her out of town to the west, and through an impressively flat and lengthy grassy field. Where the field ended, the forest began with massive oaks soaring high into the sky. The trees on the outermost edge grew in a perfectly straight line. They expanded endlessly in either direction forming a formidable wall of wood and leaves.

Beyond the tree line, the thick canopy blocked the sunlight, and an eerie blue glow filled the shadows. Rhett stopped a step away from one of the tall oaks.

"You've got your sword? Pull your hood up." He fussed over her like a mother making sure her child was ready for school.

Cassie patted the sword at her side, and quickly pulled the hood of her heavy cloak over her head. She had gotten the black velvet cloak as a gift from Rhett this morning, as a way to hopefully hide the fact that she was human in case they were seen by anyone in the forest. She was thankful for the thick fabric that cut the bitter chill of early morning, and for the luxurious-feeling red silk that lined the inside of the garment.

At the hem of the cloak that rested near her knees, tiny, swirling symbols were sewn into the velvet with red thread. At first she assumed they were just decoration, but then she got the feeling they were something more.

"They're Sigils," Rhett had explained as she examined them, "the Queen Lysette is a skilled garment maker—she's the one who gave me this cloak—and she sews a little magic into each piece of clothing. These Sigils help make the wearer a bit less noticeable and a bit more lucky while on a long journey."

Now, standing at the edge of the forest, Rhett spoke not of luck and good magic but of the dangers that might find them during their walk to his aunt's home.

"If you don't already know, there are only a few things you have to remember when walking through the forest of the Fae," he explained, "number one, be ready to grab your sword at a moments notice. The Fae can get carried away, sometimes."

As soon as they crossed the tree barrier, the temperature instantly dropped several degrees. Cassie shivered as they started down the narrow dirt path that cut through the tree line. At first, she hadn't even seen the path, as it was so overgrown with a plumage of greenery. It was the sort of path that only someone with prior knowledge of it would be able to find.

Cassie soon realized the pale blue light she had seen before was coming from the various bioluminescent fungi that sprung up from the dirt and the lichen that covered fallen trees.

Some of the mushrooms were taller than Cassie, their stems bowing under the weight of their wide, flat caps. Others grew in small bunches while some were tall and skinny with tiny rounded caps.

They were the only source of light here, casting a blueish glow on everything around. Though the light had seemed eerie from the field, Cassie was now finding it relaxing; charming, even. In fact, it was so intense, it made Rhett's hair appear to be a whimsical tint of purple.

She found herself smiling while her eyes followed firefly-sized lights that blinked in and out of existence. She wondered absently if they were in fact small insects or maybe just tiny Pixies making their way through the trees.

The forest certainly was beautiful, Cassie thought, wishing she had a camera so that she could capture the brilliance of the woods around her. For a moment, Cassie felt at ease.

Unfortunately, the feeling didn't last long.

Rhett and Cassie had been silently walking, the only sound was the crunching of debris under their feet. She had been focusing on the constant rhythm of their steps when a third set of footsteps joined in. She had started to turn her head, hoping she wouldn't find someone lurking behind them, when Rhett reached over, putting an arm around her shoulders, keeping her in place.

"Careful, you don't want to turn around."

A feeling of dread ran up her spine, sinking down into her stomach like a rock. Her voice shook as she whispered, "what's back there?"

"Odds are there's nothing there, but the Fae can make you hear things, just to scare you."

"Things?"

"Yes, like footsteps, bells or laughter... but you'll be fine as long as you don't turn around to investigate. If you look behind you while you're in here, the forest in front of you might not be the same when you turn back around. Just keep moving forward, no matter what."

He had no sooner finished relaying his warning when she heard the chime of distant bells. If Cassie hadn't known what was behind the musical tones, she would have found amusement in listening to what sounded like a symphony of a hundred wind chimes blowing in the leaves above.

Rhett tightened his grip on her shoulders. He sighed and muttered, "stay close."

"They aren't exactly harmful though, are they?" Cassie asked, remembering stories Grandma Charlotte used to tell her, "my grandma always told me they were mischievous and annoying on their best days, but that was the extent of it, I thought."

Rhett stifled a scoff, trying to be polite, "perhaps when your grandma was younger that was true. Now, especially with a war brewing, the Fae are certainly dangerous and cunning, too."

The way his eyes scanned the trees with caution reminded her of the first night she met him as he led her and Emily through the dark streets of Lark's Valley like a cat on the prowl.

"There have been multiple reports of human disappearances in the past few months. The search parties went missing as well. Eventually we discovered one of the largest Faerie revels any of us had ever seen. Most of the people were nearly starved to death by the time we got there, and the others weren't in much better condition. And, honestly, getting stuck in a revel might be the least of your worries when it comes down to it."

Cassie didn't have to ask what a revel was. She was beginning to remember some of the more grim stories her grandma would tell and shivered at the thought.

"I thought everyone knew not to go into a revel, though. How did something happen on such a large scale like that?"

"The Fae mess with your head," he said, solemnly, "if a human isn't consciously trying to block out Fae mind games, they can really alter your sense of reality. Especially their Queen. Stories say she's so powerful, she can actually fully control other people if she wanted to."

Cassie shuttered. This pleasant walk in the woods was quickly becoming less and less relaxing. Perhaps it was simply all the dark talk or maybe her subconscious was trying to tell her something, but Cassie couldn't stop the memories of her grandmother's warnings from demanding her full attention.

"Cassie, darling," Grandma Charlotte would always begin gently, tracing the backs of her bony fingers along Cassie's small cheek, "if ever you get lost during one of our walks in the woods there's a few things you must always remember."

Even walking in the woods now with Rhett Cassie could still hear her grandma's voice as if she were walking beside her, "you remember what I told you about Faerie rings? Yes, the mushroom circles, that's right, darling. If you see one never *ever* step inside of it. Faeries hold their revels in those rings, my dear, and if you enter one they will make you dance and dance until you can't dance any more. When you get hungry or thirsty, they will only feed you their food and their water, but if you take it, never again will you want human food. And please, my love, if you find anyone else wandering the woods, run straight home. Promise?"

Cassie remembered wondering why dancing and eating food would be such a bad thing. Now she knew the truth; even in the nonmagical world, Grandma Charlotte had worried for her granddaughter's safety. She had still worried about the powers of the Fae, even when she'd tried so hard to be out of reach.

Lost in her thoughts, Cassie didn't notice when the bells stopped ringing. Rhett picked up his pace, hurrying Cassie along. She looked up at him, his focused and nervous expression made her gut flop anxiously.

Her fingers fiddled with her grandmother's key around her neck. She tried to keep her composure by forcing a smile, "last night I could've sworn you said this wouldn't be dangerous," she kept her tone teasing and light, "so why do I get the feeling we're running from something?"

He turned back with a smile that brought out the dimple in his cheek. Squeezing her hand once he said confidently, "don't worry, I'll keep you safe."

The bells began to jingle in a manner that reminded Cassie of laughter. As if the Fae were saying, *we'll see about that.* Cassie pulled her hood down tighter against her head as the wind picked up, whipping their hair around and rustling the leaves on the trees.

They were walking along the edge of a steep hillside that sloped downward into a muddy creek. Knowing one wrong step would send her tumbling, she focused on where Rhett placed his own feet and followed suit.

As if acting on its own will, a towering tree in front of them leaned to the side, uprooting itself with a deep groan. As it fell, the thick root swung itself out, aiming to sweep Rhett and Cassie down into the creek. Rhett acted swiftly, shoving Cassie out of the way sending her back-first into another massive oak tree. The swinging tree root caught Rhett in the stomach, flinging him through the air and into the murky water.

Rhett clamored to his feet, soaking wet. Even though he was shouting as loud as he could, Cassie almost couldn't hear him over the gale, "stay there— coming—get you!"

Cassie had every intention of doing just that—staying put—but it appeared the forest had other plans for her. The ground began to shutter, a rumbling coming from deep within the earth. Cassie reached for her sword at her side, ready to defend herself if needed, when the forest below her erupted in waves, not unlike those that crashed in the ocean.

She tumbled and fell backward, trying to steady herself and find something stable to hold on to. With each wave she was being taken further and further away from Rhett. She screamed for him, but heard nothing in return.

After countless somersaults, a few scrapes and a few more bruises, the forest settled itself down, placing Cassie in the middle of a bare grassy clearing surrounded only by the looming trees. Only a light breeze sifted through the leaves and the sun shone high and warm in the sky.

Cassie's breath was coming in quick pants, her eyes wildly scanning the tree line for any sign of a threat. She had unsheathed her sword and was holding it out in front of her, waiting for the next surprise attack. When it did not come, she warily straightened up and took a deep breath, but kept her sword at the ready, just in case.

"Rhett!" She called in vain, knowing there was no way he'd be able to hear her now.

She was silent then, in the middle of the field trying to plan out her next move. Frustrated and fearful tears burned behind her eyes. She blinked them away angrily. Crying wouldn't help her find Rhett and it certainly wouldn't help her get out of this forest either.

"Cassidy..." Aa whisper blew over her with the breeze.

Cassie stiffened, breathing quietly but making no other noise, waiting to see if she had truly heard her name.

It came again with the east wind, "Cassidy... this way..."

The voice was neither male or female and yet it sounded familiar, like the call of an old friend. It spoke softly, summoning Cassie back into the forest.

With her sword in hand, repeating her offensive spells in her mind so as not to forget them if she needed them, Cassie started in the direction of the voice.

As she made her way deeper into the forest once again, she kept her senses on high alert, ready for anything the Fae might throw at her. With every step the voice grew louder, calling her name, beckoning her closer, farther, deeper into the wood. She began to run, desperate to find the source of the noise with an eagerness like no other.

The trees had begun to thin again, and the ground was getting softer. Cassie's feet began to sink a bit with every step. She quickly realized she was heading into a swamp when the grass beneath her feet slowly became mud. She didn't stop. Not even when the mud became muck and the muck became a dark brown water that splashed her as she barreled forward.

For a moment the ground became visible again, as the swamp floor began to slope upward. Only a few steps further ahead, she came to the edge of a terribly out-of-place little pond filled with crystal clear water.

The voice had vanished as suddenly as it had appeared and only then did she stop running. From the muddy banks of the small, circular pond, Cassie could see a mound of land that rose from the very center of the water. On that island sat a stone structure, resembling a turret that might be at the top of a castle tower. The voice had still not returned and Cassie was no closer to finding it's owner. Nevertheless, it had led her here, to this pond and the small stone turret.

The pond wasn't very deep but neither was it shallow enough to walk through. With a sigh, Cassie abandoned her heavy cloak in the mud and returned her sword to its sheath. Without wasting another minute, Cassie dove into the pond, her chest tightening in the cold water. She pulled herself up onto the little island, clearing the length of the pond after only a few strokes through the water.

As Cassie took a moment to wring out her soaked t-shirt, she heard a rustling from inside the turret. She took a curious step forward, and then another, until she heard an anxious whimper followed by a small, high voice.

"Oh dear, oh my. Not good. Not good at all." It wasn't the same voice that had led her here, but it piqued her curiosity all the same. Cassie crept to the window peering over the ledge.

Pacing along the gravelly floor was a very small man, only standing two—maybe three—feet high. His unwrinkled and rosy face suggested he was quite young, but his floor-length gray beard offered evidence to the contrary. He nervously gnawed on the fingernails of one hand while he tugged at his long, pointed hat with the other.

"What do I do?" He threw his head back in exasperation, catching sight of Cassie in the window and letting out a terrified yelp.

Cassie gasped, falling to her backside then scrambling to her feet. She hurried around to the doorway of the turret, finding the small man scurrying towards the wall, pressing his back against the cold stone.

"Don't hurt me!" He yelped.

Cassie held her hands palm out, "I mean you no harm!" She said quickly, "I just need help."

The tiny man stayed where he was but stopped looking for an exit, "help?" He parroted.

"Yes, I'm lost." Cassie said honestly.

He groaned dramatically, "lost!" He began chewing on his nails once again, "I've lost something as well."

"Is that why you're so upset?" Cassie knelt down to get closer to his level.

He turned to her then, a fearful look in his eyes, "yes, oh, I've lost something very important. Very important."

"What was it?"

"I can't tell you," he whispered.

"Could you tell me your name?" Cassie spoke in a low, calming voice.

He hesitated, "you can call me Walt."

"Walt," Cassie smiled, "I'm Cassie."

Walt visibly relaxed slightly then, "your name is safe with me."

"Safe?"

"Yes, you know, you should really be more careful which Fae you choose to give your name to, some would use its power against you if given the chance."

"Oh." Cassie said softly, "but you're not like that, are you Walt?"

"No, no, I'm not like the other Gnomes of my village. Not at all, no, they would never have lost the Queen's Memory Stone!"

Walt gasped, jumping and clasping his hairy hands over his mouth, "oh dear, oh no. I wasn't supposed to say that! Can I do nothing correctly today?"

"It's okay Walt," Cassie did her best to calm the poor Gnome, "it will be okay. I'll help you find the stone and I won't tell anyone you lost it. Would that make you feel better?"

Walt sniffled, "you would do that for me? A Gnome you just met?"

"I'd help anyone that needed my help if I were able," she smiled brightly, standing tall, "now, what does this stone look like, Walt?"

Walt began to pace again, "I shouldn't have been touching it. It's just, today's my first day, and I'd never seen a memory stone before... it was so perfectly round, and smooth... so beautiful!"

"What color was it, Walt? And how big?" Cassie began to scan the ground which was littered with rocks of all shapes and sizes.

"The other Gnomes didn't want to let me do guard duty today... no, they said, 'Walt's too scatterbrained, he can't be trusted' and trusted I shouldn't have been!" He shuttered, "Oh! Whatever will they do to me?"

"Walt." Cassie snapped her fingers, "focus. Color and size, Walt."

"Oh it's not one color, it's all the colors. Every color imaginable. So beautiful... fit perfectly in the palm of my hand..."

Looking at Walt's quivering hands, Cassie estimated this stone must be about the size of a golf ball, perhaps a bit bigger. If it was truly so colorful as Walt had described, it shouldn't be so hard to find, Cassie thought, considering the mundane grays, browns, and other natural colors of the stones in the turret.

Cassie crawled on her hands and knees, searching the small circumference of the turret that was otherwise empty besides herself, Walt, and a million rocks on the ground.

"What is a Memory Stone, anyways, Walt?" Cassie asked curiously.

"Interesting that you don't know," Walt began, "they are quite common among the Fair Folk, though, I'd imagine not as common among humans, what with your short life spans and all."

"Our life spans? What does that have to do with it?"

"The Fae live for hundreds of years in a lifetime, and sometimes it can be hard to remember everything you've experienced in such a long span of time. So, they use Memory Stones to hold a copy of some of their best memories so that they can relive them whenever they want, just in case they forget them one day."

Cassie mused on this concept for a while. If this was the Queen's Memory Stone, and she had guards in shifts protecting it in the middle of a turret in a remote swamp, it must hold something important.

"If only I could use a Memory Stone... there are so many things I'd love to always remember." Walt sighed.

"Why can't you use them?" Cassie wondered aloud.

"Well, Gnomes are immune to their magic." Walt said simply, "that's why we make the best guards. We can hold the stone in our hands all day long and never see the memories they hold."

"So all you have to do is hold a stone and you can see the memories? If you're not a Gnome, that is?"

Walt stopped pacing then, staring directly at Cassie, "if you find the stone, you mustn't touch it, Cassie. I'll really be in trouble then!"

While Cassie did feel bad for this panicked Gnome, her objective of getting out of the forest had just been replaced with finding this stone and discovering whatever secrets the Fae Queen was trying to hide. Who knew what memories the Queen would want to keep so hidden? What advantage would this give humanity in their battle for freedom here? Perhaps Cassie would discover the key to getting her family back onto the throne of Lark's Valley. Her mind reeled with possibilities.

A glint of light caught Cassie's attention, and she spun around, looking out beyond the doorway and into the water. There, at the bottom of the slope, resting alone on the sandy bed of the pond, was a stone no larger than a small kiwi fruit. Even in the distortion of the water, Cassie could see this stone was perfectly smooth.

If she had any doubts that this was in fact the Queen's Memory Stone, they were instantly dissolved as ashe saw the multitude of colors that swirled around the stone's surface. Together they formed a rainbow comprised of colors that Cassie didn't even have names for.

Walt followed her as she dashed outside and into the cold water. "Cassie!" He called worriedly, but it was too late.

Cassie had already dove under the surface, her auburn hair swirling out around her as she expelled the air in her lungs so she could sink further down. Arm extended and aimed for the stone, she started wondering what it would feel like to relive someone else's memories.

Her fingertips brushed the smooth, cold surface of the Memory Stone and curled inward, pulling the stone into the palm of her hand. The instant her hand fully clasped around the stone, everything went black.

The sun filtering down through the water had disappeared, the world around her filling with shadows. Cassie couldn't see or hear a thing, and the feeling of weightlessness in the water around her added to the supernatural sensation. For a moment, Cassie panicked, wondering if something was wrong; nothing was happening, everything was just... nothingness.

Only a moment later, she began to feel as if a drain in the bottom of the lake had been pulled, swirling, dragging her under. Still holding the stone in her hand, she clawed upward, trying to escape the whirlpool carrying her to depths unknown.

~ Thirteen ~

Finally the water stopped churning and the world around her became still. An instant later she hit the bottom, hard. She fell to her back, her teeth nearly rattling in her head. She shut her eyes tightly, waiting for the pain of the fall to come—it didn't.

Instead she felt the warmth of the sun on her skin and the gentle caress of something ticking her body. The scent of dirt and fresh air and grasses filled her nose. Warily, she began to open her eyes, wincing at the bright sun.

The laughter of children soon broke the peaceful silence, and Cassie felt herself jolt upright, her eyes springing open. The oddest part, however, being that she did not will these actions herself.

No, her body seemed to act of its own volition, and continued to do so as her head turned toward the sound, looking out over tall grasses that she had been laying in. A forest lay behind her and in front a tiny village was nestled in the distance.

A pair of children had run up to her, giggling and laughing but Cassie did not share their joy. She felt deep down that she had done something wrong. She felt a mixture of worry, shame, and fear.

I knew I shouldn't have come... the thought that flew through her mind was not her own, nor was the one that followed: *the human world is dangerous; they warned me. How could I be so careless?*

She couldn't will herself to move; she was rooted in place with fear. The two little boys were getting closer with every step, until finally they lifted their heads and spotted her.

In Cassie's own mind she noticed how peculiarly they were dressed, in clothes from a few centuries ago. Again, a thought filled her head that came from someone else. More of an instinct than a thought really, but it was telling her to run, and she felt herself turn to do just that when the little boy in front called out.

"Wait! Please! We won't harm you!" His accent was heavy and definitely English.

Cassie stopped and turned to see the boys staring bewildered at her.

"What do you want?" Her voice came out high and anxious, sounding like someone else entirely.

"What are you?" The second boy asked.

Cassie felt her chin tilt upward, her voice sounding strong and confident, "I am known by many names, for I am the keeper of nature, the product of the earth and heir to the Faerie throne in a magical land far from here. You may call me, Gaia."

"Your majesty." The first and older boy bowed gracefully. The second took a step backward, a worried look on his face.

"Jeremiah," the scared boy whispered, "I want to go home."

"Then go home, Daniel." Jeremiah kept his eyes fixed on Cassie—or was she Gaia, the Fae Queen?— "Mother will have made supper by now, I'll be along shortly."

"Step no closer, human." Gaia's voice came quivering out of Cassie's lips.

"I won't hurt you," Jeremiah promised, "my name is Jeremiah Larken. You're a real Faerie, aren't you?"

Gaia didn't answer before Cassie's world went black again as the memory ended. The world fell out from underneath Cassie but she stayed floating in the nothingness once more as she had when she first grasped the Memory Stone.

She took a moment to get her bearings, realizing that she would be experiencing these memories through the Fae Queen's eyes. It was quite the disorienting sensation, being fully immersed in sights, sounds, dialogues and feelings as if they were your own, but being unable to control the actions in any way.

She only had time for the single thought before she was launched into the next memory that the stone held. The feeling of falling, being pulled downward, washed over her again, until her feet were planted firmly on the ground.

This time, Cassie's eyes opened to a dark forest illuminated by the silver light of a full moon. A babbling creek harmonized with the breeze in the leaves and the crickets hidden in the grasses.

She could feel Gaia's impatience but it was overpowered by a sense of worry mixed with anxiety blended with a touch of eagerness. A moment later Cassie realized Gaia was waiting for someone, and they were late.

She turned around, glancing at her reflection in the running water. Gaia's face peered back, her perfectly shaped eyebrows scrunched inward a bit with anxiety. Gaia looked younger here than the mural Cassie had seen in town the other day, but she felt older than she had been in the last memory.

A worry pounded through her mind: *has he grown tired of me? Is that why he stays away?*

So, Gaia was meeting a lover here tonight. Cassie started to become impatient as well, wanting to see just who it was she was waiting for.

A crunch of leaves and twigs made Gaia whirl around. Cassie felt her mouth burst into a smile, relief filling her body as she laid eyes on a handsome young man who reciprocated the same excited smile.

"Jeremiah," Gaia had meant to sound scolding but only sounded teasing instead, "how dare you keep your Queen waiting?"

Jeremiah, Cassie realized quickly, was the same boy from the other memory but nearly ten years older here. He had grown into a dashing gentleman, with striking blue eyes and reddish hair. Strong too, by the looks of it, with muscles bulging under his overcoat.

Cassie's suspicions about his strength were confirmed as he reached forward, wrapping Gaia in his arms.

"Oh yes," he said, recalling a previous conversation, "the coronation. How did it go?"

"Without a flaw," Gaia nuzzled her face into his shoulder, "wish you could have been there."

"I wish I could have too, my darling. In fact," Jeremiah released Gaia from the embrace, but held onto her hand, walking along the path, "I wanted to talk to you about that."

Gaia was confused, "about what?"

"The magic you've been showing me, well, I've showed a few friends what I know, they showed a few people as well and so on.... Gaia," Jeremiah's voice had turned pleading as he looked her in the eyes, "we're in danger. The town officials, they've started calling us witches, they've started capturing and killing anyone who practices magic."

"Why?" Gaia's voice came out in a whisper.

"They don't understand how beautiful it is and what they can't explain, they don't want to—"

"No," Gaia cut him off, her voice rising in anger, "I meant, why would you share magic with other people?"

Jeremiah took a step back, stunned, "I—they needed help. People here... they needed magic in their lives. It's—"

"—not for you to decide!" Gaia yelled, "I wasn't even supposed to teach *you* the secrets of magic and now half of your village knows!"

"Gaia, sweetheart, please, I need your help."

"Jeremiah Larken..." she began, but her anger faded as she looked into his desperate eyes, "what do you need?"

"Take us with you," Jeremiah begged, "take us to your home, where we can live and practice magic freely. Let us leave this village and its narrow minded inhabitants behind. Let us never return to this world without magic."

"I—I can't do that."

"You're Queen now, you can do whatever you'd like!"

They were silent for a moment, and Cassie knew at this moment that this was how it happened. This was how magic came to her world, and how humans came to Lark's Valley.

This Jeremiah Larken, he was the first magical Larken, but Cassie herself was proof that he would not be the last. Perhaps it was because Cassie had a front row seat to Gaia's thoughts, or perhaps it was simply that she was living in the future that Jeremiah had created, but Cassie knew what Gaia's answer would be before she spoke the words.

"Bring the others here tomorrow night," Gaia pulled her hand out of Jeremiah's and turned to walk away, calling back quietly, "I'll take you there."

Cassie had no blackout before the next memory began. Or, rather, the next string of memories. The world before her shuttered, the scene going out of focus, blurring as if being seen through a pair of glasses meant for someone with much worse eyesight.

Cassie flew through the next memories, like a ghost, a silent observer hovering in the corner of the room.

A flash—buildings being erected in what would soon be Lark's Valley, Jeremiah standing by proudly while Gaia smiled, a nervous face under the mask of support she was trying to wear for Jeremiah.

Another flash—a middle-aged Jeremiah standing at the edge of the path leading into the Forest of the Fae where Casie and Rhett had been only a short while earlier. Gaia emerged from the shadows under the trees looking as though she may be holding back tears.

"Gaia," he tells her, "the people want me as their leader, we should rule together, with you at my side we could—"

"With *me* at *your* side?" Gaia said, disgusted, "Jeremiah Larken this has gone too far. You mustn't forget who brought you here, who bestowed the gift of magic on you, who it is that reigns here. *I* am *your* Queen."

Jeremiah's face tightened, his voice raising in anger, "you will always be my Queen, but I am *their* King."

Cassie was blown into the next sequence of memories by a gale of wind. Everything was silent, like watching a movie with the sound off and no captions, the drone of the wind drowning out every other noise.

She watched Gaia and Jeremiah arguing followed by Gaia throwing a necklace Jeremiah gave her into a lake. Another gust of wind and she witnessed Jeremiah being crowned king by the humans of Lark's Valley.

Cassie was being thrown everywhere as the storm raged—she saw, as if through a time-lapse video where everyone moved ten times faster than a normal speed, the town growing and expanding and its people becoming more powerful by the day.

The tornado she had been caught up in let her down gently then, placing Cassie into another full memory she witnessed through Gaia's eyes once more.

It was quickly obvious to Cassie that she was intruding on a particularly private memory. The Queen stood, naked, admiring herself in a full length mirror. The black tattoos covering her arms and legs snaked around her torso and abdomen as well.

"I am beautiful, powerful, merciful," she turned, facing a spacious four-post bed made from twisted tree roots where a naked Fae man lay covered only by a moss blanket, "even when the Larkens do not deserve my mercy."

"You still love him." The Fae man stated. He didn't sound angry or jealous, but confident in his statement.

Gaia stood quiet for a moment, twirling a curl of her snowy locks in her fingers. She spoke then with a bored tone, as if relaying the time to an inquiring stranger, "did you hear King Larken,"—she spat the words— "is expecting his first child with that ugly woman he calls his 'wife'?"

"So they say."

Gaia ignored him, heading for a lichen-speckled wardrobe in the far corner of the room. She threw it open, reaching her hand inside and pulling out a long, blood red robe which she tied loosely over her thin frame.

Leaving the Fae man without another word, Gaia threw open the bedroom door, storming out into the hall. She walked down a narrow corridor and up a spiraling staircase stopping only for a moment to open a heavy wooden door.

"Ah," breathed an old, hunched Fae woman that sat in the room behind the door, "my Queen. What brings you here at such a late hour?"

The room was humbly decorated with only a cot, a wardrobe and a table with a few wooden stools. Some dried herbs were strung up here and there. Jars, books, and artifacts lined the shelves of a crooked little bookcase. Gaia entered the room and perched herself on one of the stools, her robe spilling out behind her like a river of wine.

"Prophetess, I no longer wish to live in the shadow of the lark. Tell me what I must do to ascend the Larken's throne."

The old crone's eyelids closed then, opening to reveal nothing but solid white eyes, "you will have the Larken's seat, be patient, they won't be hard to defeat. Not but two hundred years will it take, for the Larkens to learn of their fate. Once a few generations of humans turn to dust, the crown they wear will surely rust. And while they sit to moan and weep, you will claim what it is you seek."

Having heard enough to satisfy her, Gaia stood to take her leave. She made it two steps toward the door when the crone spoke again, "but beware, my Queen, for there will come a female pair of royal Larken heirs. Together they will end your reign, and never will you return again."

The old Fae prophetess stumbled forward, her eyes returning to their normal chestnut brown color. Gaia took an enraged step toward her.

"You said I'd have the throne, and now you're saying it will not be mine forever?"

"Together the girls will bring upon the end of this world as we know it and the beginning of a new era in which the Fae live under their rule. It is as the prophecy tells, and my Queen, you must know the prophecies are never wrong."

"Together," Gaia repeated the word, tasting it on her tongue, "*together* the girls will bring us to an end but separately... if they are separated, we might have a chance."

The old crone looked deeply saddened, "my Queen, it is not ever a good idea to attempt to alter your fate. You would be wise to make the best out of the path you are given, not—" the woman was launched into the air then by an invisible force that held her there as she writhed and squirmed, trying to free herself.

"My Queen," she choked.

Cassie felt Gaia's lips curl into a devilish smile as she extended her arm, willing the woman higher into the air until she was pressed flat against the ceiling. "And you, dear prophetess," Gaia hissed, " would be wise to refrain from telling me what to do."

~ Fourteen ~

Cassie lay in the mud, soaked and chilled to the bone. She coughed uncontrollably, water spewing from her lungs. Her throat burned like it never had before, and she greedily gasped breaths of precious air. She opened her eyes and slowly let her vision come into focus. It was dark, and she could see the moon peaking out from behind the trees.

"Cass?" At first all she saw was a blurry outline of bright red hair, soaked and flattened to her savior's head.

"Rhett," she sighed, relieved.

Rhett pulled Cassie up onto his lap effortlessly, gently smoothing her muddy hair out of her face, "I thought I'd lost you."

"Well you did lose me,"she chuckled weakly, and was about to ask how he had found her when Rhett lifted her chin. He stared at her for a moment before he leaned down to press his lips to hers.

At first, shock froze Cassie in place, but then she leaned in closer relishing in the warmth of his lips and his embrace. Cassie had to admit, she had wondered what kissing Rhett would be like, but she hadn't imagined this.

The two of them sat under the starry night sky, soaked and covered in mud, desperately grasping each other, wanting to get closer, kiss harder, hold tighter.

"I'm sorry," Rhett pulled away slightly, resting his forehead on hers, "I had been planning on doing that much more romantically tonight but when I saw you here alone, pale and you weren't moving..." he trailed off, shaking his head gently.

"But you found me," her voice was hoarse. She lifted her shaky hand to hold the side of his face.

"You're freezing, Cass," Rhett began to stand, still holding her in his arms, "we've got to get you out of here."

"Where are we going?"

"My aunt's house is closer than Lark's Valley at this point. We should be there in just under half an hour if the Faeries don't decide to intervene again."

"How are you not getting tired of carrying me?" She teased, "I know you're strong and all, but—"

"I packed an endurance potion Grant made for me, just in case, and I'm glad I did."

They walked silently for a moment until Rhett spoke up, "what happened to you? After we got separated."

Cassie curled her arms around Rhett's neck, "I don't know if you'll believe it when I tell you."

"Try me."

"Rhett, it was so bizarre. After the forest carried me away, I heard a voice calling me. It led me to that pond and that turret where I met the strangest little Gnome—"

"A Gnome?" Rhett echoed, "what was he guarding?"

Cassie paused "how did you know he was guarding something?"

He shrugged, "that's just what Gnomes do. They are guardians of trinkets and treasures for many people."

Cassie took a breath, it still hurt to talk, but slowly she began again, "he was guarding something important all right. I assume you know what a Memory Stone is?"

Rhett looked down at her then, stopping for a moment before continuing forward, "I do."

"Well," Cassie smiled, excited to finally know more than Rhett about something, "it was the Fae Queen's Memory Stone."

At this, Rhett did stop walking. "Did you touch it, Cass?"

"That's why I had to dive in the pond, it was at the bottom. I grabbed it and, Rhett, you won't believe what I saw."

"Don't tell me here," he started to jog lightly, Cassie still in his arms, "wait until we get indoors."

It was only then that Cassie looked around them. They were out of the swampy area and back under the thick canopy of leaves. For the most part, the path was illuminated by the light coming from the mushrooms, big and small. But further in the woods, the shadows moved. Cassie wished more than anything that she hadn't felt so weak, so vulnerable, while creatures and dangers lurked around them.

Then, a short distance away, a yellow light flickered in the darkness. Slowly, a modest cob house came into view, a warm and inviting light glowing in the round windows. The curved, dark wooden door opened as they approached and a short, rounded Fae woman came out, her purple hair streaked with silver that shone in the moonlight.

"Rhett! What happened? I was worried. What's wrong with your friend?" Her voice was high and clear.

"Aunt Mags," Rhett said, relieved, "so sorry we're late, we had a bit of a... detour."

"In, in," she shooed Rhett through the doorway, "come in before you catch your death of cold!"

The inside of Aunt Mags's house was indeed warm, and smelled pleasantly floral, like lavender. The majority of the decor and furniture —as well as Aunt Mags herself—was a happy shade of purple. If

Cassie hadn't been half drowned, frozen and exhausted, she would instantly have felt relaxed and at home.

Rhett set Cassie on the long purple velvety couch and sank into the cushion next to her. "I hate to intrude," he began, "but if possible could Cass and I stay the night? Things haven't really gone as planned today and I don't think we can make the trip home."

"Nonsense," Aunt Mags settled in a chair across the room, "you needn't even ask. Of course you're welcome here. Now, tell me what happened."

Rhett gave a quick summary of events, Cassie noticed he decided to leave out the part about the Gnome and the Memory Stone and wondered why he wouldn't want Aunt Mags to know about it.

"After I found her on the edge of the pond, we hurried here and luckily the forest left us alone this time."

"I see." She tutted disappointedly, "family can't even come to visit without being attacked. The world we are living in... this war... I tell you, the end can't come soon enough. Oh," Aunt Mags jumped up, "it's quite late. I should show you to the spare room."

"I know where it is, Aunt Mags," he stood, crossing the room and planting a kiss on her cheek, "thanks again."

Cassie stood, wobbling on her feet, "thank you," she croaked, smiling softly at Aunt Mags.

Aunt Mags smiled and patted her on the shoulder, "to bed now dear, we'll be introduced properly in the morning. There are clean bed robes in the trunk by the foot of the bed," she called as Rhett and Cassie shuffled down the hallway, "extra fire wood by the hearth!"

Holding Cassie firmly by the waist, Rhett led her to the end of the dim hallway where he opened a small door with tiny violets painted on the wood.

Inside the furniture and décor were very minimalistic. An empty fireplace sat on one wall, a bed was placed in the middle of the room with a large trunk at the end of it as Aunt Mags had said, and a tall wardrobe filled the space along the other wall. The walls had hand-painted violets that matched the ones on the bedroom door.

Cassie stood awkwardly in the doorway while Rhett went to start a fire, placing a few logs in the hearth and casting a small spell to send them ablaze. After that, he went to unpack the trunk, tossing two incredibly old fashioned night dresses on the bed along with extra pillows and blankets.

"Sorry there's only one bed," Rhett glanced back at her, "I'll take the floor," he grabbed one of the night dresses and stared at it for a moment with a disappointed look, "I'm not excited about having to wear a dress," he joked. "I'll leave you alone for a moment. I have to go talk to Aunt Mags quickly, I'll be right back," he headed for the door, stopping briefly to turn back to Cassie, "you okay? You look upset."

She smiled back at him, "not upset, just surprised. Your aunt's house looks so... human."

Rhett chuckled, "I think that's part of what I always liked about it too," he latched the door shut as he stepped into the hall.

Alone, Cassie went to stand by the fire. She sat, cross legged on the wooden floor where she closed her eyes and soaked in the heat. She focused on the feeling of the fire's energy, using it to cast a simple spell to make the flame burn hotter. She then harnessed the energy buzzing in her topaz ring to conjure up a slight breeze, pulling the warm, dry air from the fire and circulating it around her.

Satisfied with her magical blow-dryer, Cassie pulled her dry shirt off, turning it inside out and using the fabric to rub the dried mud off of her face and arms. She quickly threw the hair tie from around her wrist into her hair, and slid the oversized night dress over her head.

Cassie thanked the fire and the air elements for their help before burrowing under the covers on the bed. After lying her head on the pillow, the door creaked open and Rhett popped in, wearing his own night dress.

"How do I look?" He spun theatrically.

Cassie giggled, "very handsome," she patted the bed next to her, "you don't have to sleep on the floor tonight, Rhett. This bed is plenty big enough."

Rhett hesitated but accepted Cassie's offer and took the spot next to her in bed. With the covers pulled up over their shoulders, the two of them laid on their sides facing the middle of the bed and each other.

"I had Aunt Mags send a message to the Larkens to let them know that we are okay."

"Oh I hadn't even thought about them. Emily must be worried," Cassie said.

"After everything we've been through tonight, I think it's understandable to have forgotten about the others," he reached out to push a strand of hair behind her ear that she had missed, sending chills down her spine that settled, buzzing in her lower back. "Would you like to finish telling me what you saw in that Memory Stone?"

Cassie was silent for a moment, wondering where to start. Would Rhett care that the Queen brought magic to the humans? Would it matter that she was romantically involved with her ancestor, Jeremiah?

"It's a ruse," she blurted, "the prophecy, that is."

Rhett's brow furrowed, "what proph—you mean *the* prophecy?" His eyes lit up, "with... Vi and the Lost Princess?"

Cassie nodded slowly, "in the Queen's memory, she asked her prophetess how she could claim the Larken's throne. She was told that she would hold the crown, but that together, two royal twin girls would bring the end of her reign for good. The Queen was livid.

She planned the lie right then and there, to separate the twins so she could hold the throne forever."

Rhett rolled to his back, his mouth hanging open slightly in shock while he digested the information given to him. He turned his head slightly to look at Cassie once more, "Cass, you're sure that's what you saw?"

She nodded more vigorously this time, "yes," she said confidently, "that's exactly what happened."

Rhett let out a heavy exhale, "this changes everything. Literally. Everything."

"What do we do?" Cassie whispered.

"I don't know," Rhett admitted, "best to keep this to ourselves while I think of something. Cass, this is big news."

She smiled and felt herself blush in the dim firelight.

"What?" Rhett smirked back.

"You've been calling me Cass," she said, "no one calls me Cass. I like it."

Rhett rolled back on his side, sliding towards Cassie. He clasped her hands under the covers, "thank you for coming with me today. I had promised to keep you safe and I failed you. Yet here you lay, next to me. I just wanted to say thanks for that."

His face looked troubled, and Cassie longed to reach out and hold him. What was stopping her? She asked herself. Here they were, two adults, alone, and after having shared a kiss earlier, perhaps the unspoken no-touching boundary had been dissolved.

Mustering all the confidence she had, Cassie scooted a few inches closer closing the small distance between them. She ran her hand through the red hair of his that she'd come to adore, and gently pressed her lips to his. She wanted this kiss to say everything she had trouble voicing; I trust you, I forgive you, I feel safe and happy with you.

Rhett responded immediately, returning the small kiss with another of his own, his hand gravitating to her lower back where the night dress had ridden up, revealing her skin. She gasped as his fingers tickled gently there for a moment before politely tugging the fabric back down.

He broke away then, smiling down at her, "tomorrow when I officially introduce you to my aunt, I suspect I won't be simply calling you a friend anymore?"

She giggled softly, resting her head on his chest, "I would hope not, unless you kiss all of your friends like that."

He chuckled, pulling her in closer before pulling the covers higher over them, "only the beautiful ones."

~ Fifteen ~

Cassie woke up with a smile on her lips. She stretched and rolled over, finding an empty bed beside her. The covers were cold—Rhett must have been up for quite a while.

She sat up, rubbing the sleep from her eyes. A movement in the corner of the room caught her attention. Her head whipped to the side and she gasped with surprise.

"You scared me," Cassie sighed, smiling at Rhett for a moment before realizing what he held in his hands, "is that..."

Rhett shifted his weight to the front of the chair he sat in, examining the Xirilium short sword in his hands, being very careful not to touch anything other than the wooden hilt; he had just enough Fae blood running through his veins that touching the stone meant his skin would still burn.

"Yeah, it was my uncle's. Aunt Mags said she doesn't want it anymore," he nodded in Cassie's direction.

Cassie turned her head and gasped again. Another identical Xirilium sword sat propped against the fireplace, her clothes, clean and folded, lying next to it.

"That one was Aunt Mags's sword—these two were cut from the same piece of Xirilium," he stood, crossing the room to sit on the bed next to her, "they're gifts. It can't replace the loss of the raid, but two swords are better than no swords, I suppose."

She slid slowly out of bed, crawling over to the sword. Cassie could feel the vibration of the swords energy even from a few feet away, like static electricity in the air. When she reached out her hand, the electric feeling intensified.

Grasping her hand around the hilt, she held the sword high, feeling the vibration run up her arm and course through her body. Her breathing shuttered in response.

"Woah."

Rhett chuckled as he crossed the room, "we should get going," he stood, "back to the Larken's home."

"The Larkens?" Cassie asked, confused, "I thought the whole reason we came here was to follow up on leads about the ambush?"

Rhett sheathed his sword, reaching out to help Cassie to her feet, "after what you saw in that stone, the ambush doesn't matter. We've got much more important information to deliver."

Cassie took his hand, a nervous feeling rising in her stomach, "I'm worried they won't believe us."

Rhett shrugged off her anxiety, "Grant will just make us a potion that forces the user to tell the truth. You drink it, tell the story," he shrugged again, "problem solved."

Rhett might have been satisfied with that solution but it only made Cassie more upset. There was no way she could take a truth-inducing potion when she was hiding such a big secret about who she was. It was going to be hard enough to make them believe her about what she saw as it was, let alone if they knew that she was the Lost Princess.

He left her to get dressed then, and she slowly got changed. Her mind was racing and it seemed like all of her thoughts kept circling back to the same place. She didn't want to admit it, in fact, she'd take any other option instead, but she knew one thing for sure. Rhett needed to be told the truth.

Rhett needed to know Cassie was the Lost Princess. Sooner rather than later, unfortunately. That much was clear. The only question now was, how to do it?

Setting her fears aside for a moment, Cassie wandered out into the living room. She heard Aunt Mags's cheerful laughter before she saw the jolly little woman patting Rhett's smiling face. Normally, such a familial display of love would bring a smile to Cassie's lips as well, but she was in such turmoil on the inside that it made even a smirk impossible.

Rhett lifted his head as Cassie entered and had to double take, the smile falling from his face upon seeing her, "Cassie? Is everything alright?"

She forced a sheepish smile, "I'm not feeling so well this morning."

"Tea!" Aunt Mags chirped, "tea will fix everything."

Rhett reached a loving hand out, grasping Aunt Mags by her shoulder, "that does sound lovely, Aunt Mags, but we really should be going, especially if Cassie isn't feeling well."

A disappointed smile crept onto her face. She clasped her hands in front of her, "well you two will most certainly have to visit again soon so we can spend some proper time together," Aunt Mags crossed the room to stand by Cassie, "Rhett, will you make sure nothing was left in the bedroom before you're on your way?"

Rhett nodded once and obliged. Aunt Mags turned to Cassie, her purple hair pulled neatly away from her matching violet eyes that were alight with emotion.

"Dear," she began, clasping Cassie's hands in hers, "I have not seen my nephew smile in years. I may not have had a chance to get to know you while you were here, but the way he looks now, it says all I need to know."

Cassie only smiled squeezing Aunt Mags's hands—the right words evaded her. Rhett returned to the room before Cassie could summon a proper response.

"All clear. Ready to go?"

The walk out of the forest was much easier than the journey in. It was almost as if the forest had purposefully cleared a path for them. No longer did the shadows move around them nor did the sound of bells ring in the leaves. The path was clear of all debris; easily visible straight through to the field that separated Lark's Valley from the Faerie's woods.

In fact, the walk seemed much shorter today than it had when they were coming in. And yet, carrying such a heavy heart made the trek seem endless. Walking alongside Rhett with her hand hooked in the crook of his elbow and their hips knocking together with each stride would have been nice, if she didn't feel like she were about to shatter the foundation she'd been building here.

She loved magic and she adored the friends she made in Lark's Valley. She had accepted—for the most part—that she would just have to get close to her family in the way every stranger did, from afar. That would be better than never knowing them, at least. Cassie and Emily were thriving ever since they came through the portal that day. Was it worth it to lose all of the progress they'd made by revealing her secret?

Cassie knew she was being selfish. Part of her felt like she deserved a little selfishness after having the life she was born to lead taken away from her. And then, part of her wondered if telling the truth and doing everything she could to fulfill the true prophecy would give her the opportunity to have that life after all.

She could live the life of a Lost Princess returned home, and after having dethroned a cruel tyrant, therefore wining the adoration of her people, maybe she could have the family she'd always dreamed of.

On the other hand, Cassie knew this was all fantasy. Reality was death, if she revealed her identity in the wrong way. It was imperative that others believe the truth of the prophecy first before knowing who she was. Otherwise, they might think she made the whole thing up to save her own life.

Absently, she wondered what it would feel like to drink a potion that pulled the truth from your lips. Maybe that was the key—if she took the potion and assured the others she was here for good reasons perhaps they wouldn't—

"You're very quiet," Rhett's calm voice broke her away from her daydreams.

"I've got a lot on my mind," she admitted.

"You look sad," he observed.

Cassie didn't respond right away. What was there to say?

They were in the middle of the grassy field now, only a few minutes more until they reached Lark's Valley. She stopped walking, the tall grasses tickling her arms as she pulled away from Rhett.

"There's something I have to say."

He turned, meeting her gaze. Even now, with a questioning look on his face he smiled at her. The breeze blew his red hair around, a few strands falling across his eyes. She felt the words on her tongue, they sat there, just behind her lips; *it's me. I'm the Lost Princess. I didn't mean to lie to you, well, at first I did but it was only out of fear for my life and then you came along and—*

She brushed the stray hairs away from his face, "I had a really good time with you these past couple days."

"I had a good time too, but that made you sad?"

"No," she chickened out. She couldn't bring herself to say the words that so badly needed to be said, "no I wasn't sad, really. I suppose I'm just feeling a lot of things lately and..."

"It's okay," he took her hand and began walking again, "you don't have to say it. I understand."

Unless Rhett was also lying about who he was and why he was here, hiding himself from a family he wasn't allowed to know, she doubted very much that he understood. Cassie dropped the subject for now. The inevitable conversation was better suited for another time, she decided.

* * *

"Where is everyone?" Cassie took a few steps into the house. All was quiet, save the ticking of the grandfather clock.

"The memorial," Rhett said somberly, "everyone is preparing for the funeral for those that we lost in the raid that night."

"Rhett!" Annie's voice came from the top of the staircase, "thank goodness you're here."

"Cassie!" Emily's voice trailed not far behind.

As the girls descended the stairs Rhett leaned in to Cassie, whispering so only she could hear, "let's keep what we know to ourselves for now, okay?"

Cassie only had a chance to nod before being wrapped in a hug from Emily.

"I was so worried," Emily said, holding her friend at arms length, "are you okay?

Tears welled in Cassie's eyes. She pulled Emily in for another hug to hide the tears. She buried her face in Emily's shoulder, muttering, "I'm fine, but I have so much to tell you."

"Come on," Emily grabbed Cassie by the hand, walking towards the stairs, "I bet you want to get cleaned up. We don't have much time before the memorial, so you'll have to tell me all about your trip afterwards."

In Cassie's bathroom, she slowly dipped herself into the warm, bubbly bath water. Her whole body tingled with relief. She knew she couldn't linger long here but for the first time in days, Cassie took a deep breath, closed her eyes and started to relax.

Emily poked her head in the door, "I left your outfit and accessories on the bed," she said, "meet you downstairs when you're done!"

As the water began to cool, Cassie reluctantly pulled herself out of the tub, wrapping herself in a towel. Upon finding the clothes Emily had selected for her, she noticed a small, square, black box on top of the folded clothes. A gold ribbon held the lid on, and under it was a white slip of parchment.

Happy Birthday! These will look nice next to that key of yours. Love, Emily

Was it really September already? Cassie did the math and she couldn't believe it. Had she really been here for three whole months? It appeared time had flown by much faster than anticipated; she was turning nineteen today.

Slowly she had to remind herself that only she and Emily knew it was her birthday. Of course, if only she would tell Rhett the truth, then she'd have at least one more person that would know.

She wondered for a moment if Vi would be doing anything to celebrate. Then she thought about it for a moment and doubted there would be any kind of birthday celebration, since they had a much more somber event to attend instead.

Cassie slowly untied the ribbon. As she lifted the lid, her jaw dropped. Sitting in the bottom of the satin-lined box were two small pendants, each a beautiful piece of dark red Xirilium. She reached up to unclasp the chain around her neck, slipping the Xirilium pendants onto the necklace so that they rested on either side of her grand-mother's key.

Emily had picked Cassie's clothes to coordinate with her new pieces of jewelry. A sleeveless maroon top and a pair of black skinny jeans with matching maroon ankle boots.

With a quick spell Cassie dried her hair, leaving it pin-straight and smooth, falling to the bottom of her shoulder blades. She didn't bother equipping much more. The Xirilium around her neck felt like more than enough energy to cast as many spells as she might need.

Quickly, Cassie darted out of the room. Following Emily's earlier instructions, she made her way to the living room so she could head to the funeral with everyone else. The forest where Cassie had en-countered the Giant Spider was where the ceremony would be, and it was a short walk from the house.

She was doing her best to try to forget her worries, even if only for the night. Unfortunately, her best wasn't good enough. Even as she helped stack wood for the makeshift pedestals and took on every other task possible to keep her hands busy, her mind wandered.

It was impossible to think about anything else with such a press-ing matter at hand. How could she possibly put it all aside and focus? She didn't see a way. Instead of drawing attention to herself, though, she decided she would put on her best poker face and at least make it through the night.

The sun was setting and everyone was gathering in a loose crowd. Cassie wondered silently where Rhett was.

His familiar voice drew her attention to the path behind her. Rhett had his arm draped over Grant's shoulder and they were mak-ing their way towards her. She felt herself smile and her heart picked up its pace at the sight of him. Cassie met them halfway and was pleased to see Rhett's face light up as well.

They both looked awfully handsome with their button down shirts and clean, pressed slacks. Rhett's hair was pulled back, as usual. Simple Grant had his hair perfectly brushed and held in place by what Cassie would normally assume was hair gel, but knowing him it was probably just one of Grant's own recipes.

"You both look very nice," she complimented them.

Grant nodded an acknowledgment then caught a glimpse of something over Cassie's shoulder. She turned to see Vi, looking gorgeous as always in a dark navy floor-length dress. She stood tall but Cassie could see tears in her eyes even as she talked with a few friends.

"Excuse me," Grant muttered.

"I've got something for you," Rhett kept his voice low.

He grabbed her wrist and led Cassie away from the growing crowd, further into the forest.

"Where are we going?" She asked as they ducked behind a rocky hillside.

When she thought he was about to answer, he pulled her in close, his lips brushing against hers. Her heart raced and her eyes fluttered closed. She felt his lips move against hers, his hot breath tickling her face.

She pulled back to see his face, "do people usually exchange gifts at funerals here?"

"No," he admitted sheepishly, "but we have a bit before the ceremony begins," he took a deep breath, slowly exhaling before continuing, "I thought you could use a little something good in case things get bad later, when we have to tell everyone the truth about the prophecy."

"Rhett I appreciate that but, here? Now? We can't wait until—" she peered out from being the rocky ledge to see more people gathering around the pedestals.

"There's a reason memorials are held here in this particular forest," he explained, ignoring her concern, "these trees are some of the oldest in the world. Some say they've been here longer than the Faeries themselves, others say these very trees were the very first living things ever created," he lifted his head, closing his eyes slowly.

The light breeze caressed his face and blew a few stray hairs gently out of his eyes. He took a deep breath and Cassie did as well, savoring every bit of the scent that lingered here; dirt, decaying leaves, and crisp, fresh air.

"But no matter what each person believes," he said, "everyone agrees that the trees here hold a special kind of magic. Here, among the ancient wood, you can feel a connection to the world beyond the grave."

Without another word he knelt down to where a bit of the stone receded, creating a miniature cave in which the dirt of the forest floor sunk inward. He reached his hand in and pulled a round bottomed glass bottle from the secret spot.

The glass was clear and mostly empty, its contents reduced to perhaps a few tablespoons on the bottom of the bottle. The potion was thin and sparkled in the moonlight. It looked as if someone had dumped a bottle of silver glitter in water and gave it a good swirl. Rhett stared at it wistfully for a moment before uncorking it and handing the bottle to Cassie.

"This potion only works here, in this sacred place. There's only enough for one more dose. I want you to have it."

Cassie gently took the bottle, "what is it?"

"It will allow you to visit with someone you've lost, for a short time. It was my father's last masterpiece. This is the only bottle in existence; Grant and I have tried to figure out the recipe but haven't had any luck."

"Rhett, I can't accept this." Cassie tried to hand the potion back to him but he only shook his head.

"Please, I insist."

Slowly, she lifted the rim to her lips. The liquid inside had no scent but a chill rose from the bottle instead, like a draft coming from a broken window seal.

When the potion hit her tongue it felt textured and rough, but still had no taste. It chilled her throat on the way down, a line of cold spreading into her chest and stomach.

"Cassie, darling."

Cassie froze in place. The voice had come from behind her, where a second ago there hadn't been anyone. Slowly she turned, dropping the bottle in the dirt at her feet when the figure before her came into focus.

The woman standing near a tall old oak was there and yet not. Her soft, wrinkled skin was translucent—so much so that Cassie could see the leaves on the tree waving in the breeze behind her. Her gray and white hair was neatly braided back, a crocheted shawl thrown over her shoulders. A kind and familiar smile was at home on her face, and Cassie's knees began to wobble.

"Grandma?"

Rhett let out a choked sound, but Cassie couldn't look away from her grandmother for fear that she might not be there when she turned back around. He muttered something too soft for Cassie to hear, then fell to his knee beside her, his head tilted downward in respect as he faced Grandma Charlotte.

"My Queen," he said formally.

Grandma Charlotte chuckled, "my, I haven't been called that in quite some time."

"How?" Tears spilled over onto Cassie's cheeks.

"The potion, my dear," Grandma Charlotte took a few steps toward her, the ground beneath her feet undisturbed, "speaking of which we don't have much time. Mr. Daniels," Grandma Charlotte placed a transparent hand on his shoulder, "stand tall. No need for formality here."

Cassie outstretched her hand, attempting to grasp her grandmother's arm, but it fell through the air.

She sucked in a sharp breath, "are you really here?"

"Not entirely," she chuckled, "Cassie, I'm sorry to ruin our reunion with such depressing talk, but dear it's true what they say: to those beyond the grave, nothing is a secret. I now know so much more than I ever could have when I walked the earth. The truth about the prophecy... you both know as well, hm?"

Cassie was speechless. She nodded quickly once.

"Why did you keep it all from me?" She asked breathlessly.

Cassie was vaguely aware that Rhett had spoken, but didn't hear what he had said. All that mattered now was this moment. Never again would she get the opportunity to see her grandmother—not like this.

Her grandmother took a step forward, "Cassidy, I didn't have a choice. It was part of the deal; I couldn't speak a word about our past."

"Grandma, I felt so alone. I have a family here and I never knew it."

The tears wouldn't stop flowing down Cassie's cheeks. More than anything Cassie wanted her grandmother to hold her which only made her cry harder, knowing she couldn't have that.

"You have them now," Grandma Charlotte's voice was soothing, "I can't replace the years we all lost but you can live each day making the most of the ones you have left."

Her image was becoming more translucent, the trees and moon behind her becoming more visible by the second. There were so many things Cassie wanted to say and no time to say them. She settled for six words.

"I love you, Grandma. Thank you."

"I love you too," Charlotte said, her voice lingering on even after Cassie could no longer see her, "I'd do it all again for you, my little lark."

Cassie exhaled a shaky breath. Her knees felt weak and her stomach was in knots. She closed her eyes and tried to focus on her surroundings in an attempt to ground herself. The cool breeze tickled her warm face and filled her lungs as she took deep breaths.

It was only then that she realized Rhett was still standing next to her. She turned to him, tears in her eyes.

"Rhett," she whispered.

His face was hard, emotionless. His eyes searched her face though she wasn't sure what he was looking for.

Slowly he began to shake his head, "I don't understand how I didn't see it," he scoffed, "it all makes sense."

Her jaw hung open, she wanted to say more but didn't know if anything she could possibly say would be a balm for the hurt here.

"I didn't know she would come here... I didn't mean to—"

"Of course you didn't mean to out yourself," he snapped, "you've so carefully hidden your lie this whole time."

"Rhett it's not that simple."

"Seems simple to me," he began to pace. His fingers pinched the bridge of his nose and he closed his eyes, "how could I be so stupid?"

"I was afraid for my life, Rhett!" She began to raise her voice, then realized the others were still just on the other side of the rocks. It took effort to bring her shouting down to a harsh whisper, "I didn't mean to come here and then once I did, I realized everyone wanted me dead but that didn't stop me did it?"

She was starting to get angry now; her blood pressure rising as her lips curled into a snarl. How could he forget how far she'd come, how much she'd done for their cause? She may have lied, yes, but when it came down to it she had done more good than bad. Hadn't she?

"I still risked my life and did everything I could for this place," she continued, "I wanted to tell you," her voice cracked, "I was just so afraid of *this*."

He met her gaze, anger still burning behind his eyes, "this?" He echoed questioningly.

"Losing you. Losing everything I've come to know over these past few months here." She hugged her arms, feeling as if she were going to fall apart. Maybe, just maybe if she squeezed tight enough, she could hold herself together, "all of the friendships and progress I've made. I didn't want to throw it away."

They stared at each other in silence for a long while. Eventually, Cassie leaned back against the rock, feeling drained. Rhett was still staring at her, wearing a mask of hurt and anger.

"What now?" She whispered.

"I don't know." He admitted turning away from the funeral and away from Cassie, "I have to sit with this for a while. Alone." He added the last word sharply as Cassie stood to follow him.

She watched, frozen in place, as he walked back towards the Larken's home. She sobbed, silently, still holding her arms against her with all her might.

Of course her grandmother was the one that was going to appear when she took that potion; who else? What had she been thinking? Truthfully, she really hadn't been thinking anything, and now look where it had her.

This was the exact reaction she was trying to prevent by holding off on telling Rhett the truth in the first place. Hours ago they had been laughing and kissing, holding each other close and enjoying their time together, now he couldn't even look at her. How would they recover from this?

She knew she should go find Emily and explain to her what happened, together they might come up with a suitable solution. However, when her legs started moving again she did not find herself going to join the ceremony that had begun. Instead, she wandered further down the path, the cool air bringing up goosebumps on her arms.

Cassie let her tears fall freely. If she thought she had felt alone last winter when her grandmother had first passed, she really knew what it meant to be alone now.

Sure, her best friend had come with her to this world but she had thrived even more so then Cassie had. Emily had made new friends, discovered new skills, and built foundations for a new better life here.

Cassie had made a few friends, admittedly, and for a while there she thought Rhett would be a consistent part of her life. The wound that was created from having her family so unknowingly blind to the truth—blind to her and who she really was—ached with a fresh new pain.

In a haze, she wandered until the sounds and the lights from the ceremony were nonexistent. Her boots crunched the debris on the forest floor, while crickets chirped in the grass and the noises of other small animals came from above. The wind wrestled with the leaves and for a moment she felt at peace. Perhaps there really was an old magic in this forest.

172 ~ LIVVY HOLLIS

She may have been alone, but there was life all around her. Nature grew and thrived all on its own. Maybe she could be like a force of nature, powerful even when all alone.

The wind slowly quieted down, and yet Cassie noticed that the leaves still rustled. She began to feel uneasy, her moment of peace had evaporated.

Cassie stood perfectly still, wondering what was inhabiting the trees that could make them shiver so much. She went to reach for her sword, realizing with anger that she hadn't equipped it before going to the funeral.

"Who's there?" She called to the air.

She gasped when something hit her in the back of the knees, buckling her legs and sending her face first to the ground. She immediately flipped over to her back trying to sit up. In front of her, a horde of small creatures were rushing down from the trees, headed straight toward her.

She scrambled backwards, attempting to put some distance between her and whatever was approaching her. The advancing group jumped into the air, each individual creature moved so in sync that she thought for a moment it might be a singular predator. As they rose out of the shadows on the ground and into the moonlight, Cassie realized what she was looking at.

Gnomes.

She remembered too late that she had two Xirilium pendants hanging on the chain around her neck. She was unable to cast any sort of defensive spell before the horde descended on her.

Cassie screamed, but she knew no one was close enough to hear. She struggled to break free of their grasp, but dozens of tiny hands grabbed at her arms and legs. A moment later she realized they were tying together her wrists and ankles. She could no longer move more than a few inches, as they had bound her knees, thighs and torso all too well.

When she was fully and securely tied up, she rolled onto her side coming face to face with one of the larger Gnomes—by the looks of it, he was the leader of this group.

He was an old and gnarly little man, with a white beard that grew longer than he was tall, not excluding the height of his pointy hat. On his left eye he wore a black leather patch. The other eye glared right at her, his lips turned up in a sneer.

"Walter!" He called in a gravelly voice.

As the little Gnome came forward from the crowd the realization sunk in; this was no random attack. This was about the Memory Stone.

"This is the human?" The old Gnome asked.

Walt looked ashamed. His head was bowed, his shoulders slumped. He wouldn't meet Cassie's eyes as he kicked dirt back and forth with the toe of his boot. Slowly, he nodded, confirming her identity and sealing her fate.

True panic set in. Her animalistic instincts forced the last of the air in her lungs outward in a piercing shriek. She prayed that some-one—anyone—would hear her.

The Gnomes paid no attention to her cries and continued to drag her away into the shadows of the forest.

As the path she had just been on faded away, Cassie heard the old-est Gnome laugh. The sound of joy sounded out of place in the situa-tion.

"Good. 's been a long time since we 'ad a human 'n our dungeon," the evil smirk on his lips deepened into a sinister grin, "too long."

CPSIA information can be obtained
at www.ICGtesting.com
Printed in the USA
BVHW042258240221
601095BV00010B/645

9 780578 841694